I0717696

A WILD RIDE

THOMPSON & SONS: BOOK 5

VIVIAN AREND

A Wild Ride
Copyright © 2016 by Arend Publishing Inc.
ISBN: 9781989507056
Edited by Anne Scott
Cover Design © Damonza
Proofed by Sharon Muha

CHAPTER 1

July, Rocky Mountain House

A rapid, intoxicating beat filled the air as country music echoed off the wooden walls of Traders Pub. Troy Thompson eased his hands around the young woman in his arms and guided her expertly across the floor in a madcap, whirling two-step.

The sweet young thing was wrapped around him tighter than necessary, pressing her breasts to his chest as her eyes flashed with desire. The dance floor was crowded, but they didn't need to be rubbing together like two pieces of kindling.

Normally, he didn't mind when a lady made it clear that after the dance floor, she'd be game for a little dancing of the more sexual nature, but Troy was currently off the market. Had been for the past six months, which was in some ways really strange since no one knew.

No one, except him and his secret lover.

He'd never had trouble finding female company, but Troy didn't flip from bed to bed. Sticking with one woman at a time was fun enough, and made it easier to remember what things a girl liked and what she didn't.

But since January he'd been having the time of his life fucking around with Nicole Adams. It wasn't intended to be long-term or permanent on either of their parts, and the arrangement was working fine.

Nic had insisted no one else could know, *especially* not her twin brother, Mike. Who, coincidentally, was Troy's best friend and roommate.

That was one conversation he was eager to avoid.

"You're *such* a good dancer," his partner announced loud enough to be heard above the music. "And *so* strong." Her fingers squeezed his shoulder as she hummed her approval.

In answer, Troy twirled the woman faster, forcing her to cling for dear life instead of stroking him. The up-close-and-personal time with a woman who was not Nicole might help keep the gossips at bay, but he wasn't going to do anything more than enjoy the young lady's company on the dance floor.

He wouldn't drop her on her ass, but he wasn't going to get her hopes up, either.

He was already looking forward to slipping over to Nic's place later that Friday night. It seemed nobody thought anything of him dropping in at strange hours. Not with the way their families had been good friends for years.

Thoughts of Nic made him ease his grip on the woman in his arms, guiding her toward the far side of the dance floor in anticipation of the music ending.

Once this dance was over he'd be that much closer to heading out so he could go find Nicole and fuck her senseless.

Near the doorway, a woman with painted-on jeans

stood with her back to him, her heart-shaped ass drawing his eye as she spoke with some guy he didn't recognize. Her flannel shirt was tucked in tight at the waist, hips flaring wider as her jeans lovingly caressed sweet, womanly curves.

Dark hair with rich golden highlights hung to her shoulders, swinging in a blunt cut that framed the sides of her face in the brief glimpses he caught.

The music changed, and the woman in his arms gave him a *look*.

Troy forced himself to focus even as his attention kept drifting toward the door. He tucked his fingers under his partner's chin for a moment, tilting her head back. "Thanks for the dance, darlin'," he said.

"You know where to find me for another round. Any time."

Her lashes fluttered, lips pouting in invitation, but Troy just smiled good-naturedly then patted her on the ass and sent her back to the table where her girlfriends were eyeing him and giggling. Talking behind hands.

He took a quick glance toward the door, but the mysterious woman still had her back to him, leaning close to speak in her date's ear. Troy made his way across the room back to the table where his friend Mike waited, an arm draped around a familiar redhead dressed head to toe in black leather. Tessa, one of the waitresses from the café.

"You two dancing some more?" he asked, leaning an arm on the table as he looked Tessa over. Just because she was with Mike didn't mean he couldn't enjoy the view.

She eased back against Mike, jutting out one hip. "We're heading home. You want to join us?"

Oh boy. Troy glanced at Mike, but his friend shrugged at the invitation, leaving it up to him to accept if he wanted.

It wouldn't be the first time they'd had a woman between them, but it wasn't on Troy's radar at the moment.

"I'll leave you two to it," he replied. "Though I'm honoured by the offer."

"Your loss," she returned with a wink. "If you change your mind, you know where to find us."

"Hey, bro, who's the fox by the back exit door?" Troy asked before his friend could run away.

Mike turned, peering toward the door with interest. "Which one? Blonde?"

"Brunette. Wearing the fuck-me boots and—"

A fist smashed into his shoulder. "Ass."

"*What?*" Troy glanced again at the door. "I'm just saying I would—"

Damn. The woman turned to the dance floor, and Troy swallowed the words he was about to say which were something along the line of how hard he would hit that if he got a chance.

"You're such a shit. Always joking around." Mike laughed. "Yeah, I didn't recognize her at first either. I guess the new hairstyle goes with my sister's fancy job at the law office."

"Nic looks good," Troy said, wary but needing to be honest. "It suits her."

"She's my sister," Mike replied, as if that fact made her one step away from a eunuch. He wrapped his fingers around Tessa's hip and pulled her with him. "We're off. Have fun."

Troy was pretty positive he was going to have a blast. He turned to get a better view, taking in the full effect of Nicole's new look.

The shorter hairstyle was seriously professional, the front cut into a heavy set of bangs that set off her high cheekbones and narrow chin to perfection. It was a big change from her usual ponytail or braid, and combined with the makeup she wore, her green eyes were mesmerizing. Deep-red lipstick accentuated her soft, kissable lips.

Oh yeah, he was going to have a good time dropping by her place later tonight. He checked his watch, resisting the urge to march across the dance floor and take her in his arms for a spin. Nothing dirty, just a casual dance between friends—at least as far as everybody else knew.

She was already headed for the door, slipping away before temptation made him do something stupid.

Casual. That's what they'd promised each other, and that's what he'd give her until this thing between them was over. Then they'd go back to being friends, no one the wiser. No hurt feelings, no harm done.

Troy checked his watch again, calculating how long he needed to wait before he could head to her house and make both their evenings.

"House rules?" her date asked.

Nicole wasn't sure how to answer. She hadn't played Monopoly except for a few times with her family, and that had been ages ago. They hadn't cared enough to make special rules. "Tell me what rules you play by," she suggested.

Jason went into some long explanation about how no one was allowed to buy St. Charles, and if you owned two out of three properties you could put houses on them, but not hotels. Nicole nodded as he spoke, but she wasn't really listening.

First dates? Sucked.

Dinner had been great, but then she'd taken him by the dance hall. He hadn't wanted to stay at Traders for more than a few minutes, claiming it was too loud for them to talk. He'd been open to her suggestion that they should go back to her house, but...

She couldn't believe they were going to play a board game. Then again, she didn't know that much about serious dating, not with a professional guy like Jason.

She didn't know much about serious dating, period.

Until now she'd been having fun with her friends, hanging out with groups and hooking up with guys she hit it off with. No one on a regular basis, though...

No one, except Troy Thompson. They'd been fooling around on the sly for a while, which was great and wonderful because, my *God*, the man could just about make her orgasm by *looking* at her.

She was no fool—hot freaky sex on the regular with a guy who looked like Troy *and* knew where to find a woman's clit? Other than keeping it on the down-low from her family because Troy and Mike were BFFs, she'd had a blast.

Only the fling was over, and it was time to move on—

A loud crash sounded outside. They both glanced toward the back porch as another followed hard after it.

Drat—sounded as if she had unwelcome visitors.

Nicole interrupted Jason's explanation. "Hold that thought. Bet it's the neighbour's dog in the garbage cans again."

He rose halfway from his seat. "I'll help."

She waved him down. "Thanks, but I don't want to spook Pookie. Go ahead and get the game ready."

"Okay. I'll set up the bank."

She headed for the back door, a deep sigh escaping her.

Obviously she needed to adjust her expectations now that she was playing the dating game. Slow and boring seemed to be the agenda.

Stop that. He's a nice guy, her conscience poked, but all Nicole could think about was how different tonight had been compared to the last time she went out with a group of friends. They'd watched a movie then hung out. The evening had been full of laughter, lighthearted fun, and had ended with some spine-melting sex that had made both her and Troy damn happy, no strings attached…

Only she wasn't fucking around anymore. It was time to get more serious about relationships. Thus the official date.

Thus the official boredom.

God, was she *ever* going to have sex again?

She opened the back door, ready to chase off whatever was on the porch, only to be trapped by a pair of dark-brown eyes set on *smolder*.

"Hey, babe."

"Troy. What are you—?"

For a big guy, Troy moved like a panther. He had crossed the threshold in an instant, closing the distance between them and enveloping her in his arms. A second later his mouth was over hers as he took her lips in a blistering, pussy-clenching kiss.

Hot, possessive. Intense and demanding, and her reaction was instant and unstoppable. She softened under him, responding to his demands and, *oh my God,* soaking in every bit of pleasure he offered.

Her back hit the wall, and for the next few seconds, she was overwhelmed with lust. He kissed like he was craving her, and the most natural thing in the world was to kiss him back. Tongues tangling, she instinctively wrapped her legs around his strong hips as she dug her fingers into his muscular shoulders.

Time blurred, and sensation faded to the pleasure whipping through her like a runaway train. Except...there was some reason they shouldn't be doing this. Some—

Shit. She was on a date with another guy. She should most definitely not be arching into the hand Troy had shoved under her shirt, squeezing her breast possessively as a hungry growl escaped him.

She shoved back, opening enough distance between them that she could speak, quiet but insistent. "Oh my God, Troy, *stop.*"

He adjusted his grip, catching hold of her hips and grinding them together, his thick cock rubbing her aching clit through two layers of jeans still setting off fireworks.

Desire flashed in his eyes. "Two choices. Here, against the wall, or on the kitchen table. Pick."

"We're not having sex," she insisted, whispering the words.

Troy chuckled evilly. "Not yet, but give us thirty seconds and—"

"Nicole? Everything okay?"

Jason's question broke through the sexual maelstrom in the kitchen, and *finally* Troy froze.

"Everything's fine," she called as she scrambled for an excuse to keep her date in the other room, because it would be impossible to explain why she was currently in a sexually suggestive position, pinned to the wall by a man the size of a gladiator. "My...friend stopped by. I'll just be a second."

Then her feet were back on the floor, Troy holding her steady until she found her balance. He tilted his head toward the front room. "Who the hell is that?" he demanded.

Nicole squared her shoulders. "My date."

The confusion in his eyes was followed rapidly by anger. "What the fuck?"

Okay, that was too far. Annoyance replaced her temporary panic. What right did Troy have to be mad? She'd told him the fling was over. He was the one interrupting her evening. "A date? You've heard of those things?"

"Yeah, but you don't date," Troy said.

"I do now," she said sharply, more irritated by the second as she wiggled to release herself from the cage of his arms. "Go away. I need to get back—"

"Who is he?" Troy took a step toward the living room.

Nicole grabbed him by the wrist and attempted to jerk him to a stop. "Don't you dare go in there," she whispered frantically. "Troy, *no…*"

Her weight didn't slow him in the slightest as he dragged her after him down the short hallway. She recovered her footing and released him as they rounded the corner into the living room.

Jason turned toward them, surprise drifting over his features. "Oh. Hello."

A second later she had to slam on the brakes to keep from smashing into Troy. He'd stopped right in her path, his massive shoulders and torso turning him into a dandy roadblock.

God, he was such a pain in the ass. Nicole planted both hands on his back and shoved as hard as she could, which meant the big lug shifted all of two inches to one side.

Barely enough space for her to squeeze past him and offer an apologetic smile to her date. "Sorry about that. This is Troy, my brother's best friend. Troy, this is Jason."

Her date frowned slightly as if confused, which he had

every right to be, but he politely rose to his feet and held out a hand. "Jason Millette."

Troy stood rocklike, eyeing Jason as if he were a lump of leftovers forgotten in the fridge for too long.

"Troy dropped off some stuff for the family. He's not staying," Nicole announced, stepping in to push Troy toward the back door, herding him like a lost bull who'd wandered into the daisy patch.

Troy stood his ground, accepting Jason's hand. "Troy Thompson."

Nicole cringed, hoping he wasn't going to do something rude like crush Jason's hand, Troy released the other man after a sturdy handshake, but then the jerk settled in the easy chair to the side of the couch as if he had every intention of staying awhile.

"New in town?" he asked, his smile broadening. Turning on the charm.

"Just joined the law firm," Jason admitted. "Newest junior partner. You?"

"Family runs the local garage. You need a summer tune-up, let me know. We get pretty full with tourists breaking down and RV repairs, but I'll sneak you in."

"Hey, thanks for the offer. I might take you up on that. I usually do my own maintenance, or get the dealership to take care of it, but it's been pretty busy getting settled in at the new job."

"I bet." Troy leaned back comfortably, glancing at the coffee table. "Are you kidding me? Monopoly? I haven't played that in years. God, it used to kill my brothers. I'd make their lives hell every time they tried to clear that third corner. I owned Kentucky to Marvin Gardens."

Jason chuckled. "Best strategy around. Ignore the cheap

properties and Park Place/Broadway, and knock their knees out with middle-income rent and utilities."

"Ha—you can have the utilities, I get the railroads." Troy was leaning forward now, elbows on his knees, eyes sparkling as if this was the most scintillating conversation he'd had in years.

Nicole was going to freaking kill him. "Well, nice of you to drop by, but we're about to—"

"You want to play?" Jason offered. "Three is always better than two."

Only if they were talking about fooling around, which Nicole doubted. Troy had never been interested in having anyone else participate while they'd fucked before, and it wasn't likely he would start by suggesting a ménage with the newest junior member of the local law firm.

She turned and faced her annoyance directly, offering the evilest eye she could. "Troy can't stay," she announced firmly.

"Troy would love to stay," he contradicted her, dragging his chair across the floor until he was within arm's reach of the game. "I'm the race car."

"Dibs on the top hat," Jason flashed back.

Troy leaned back and winked. "Got any Coke, Nic?"

She was stuck. Complaining would only make her look like a two-year-old throwing a tantrum. But his ass was grass. "Sure, ol' buddy, ol' pal."

"In the can," he ordered. He stared at her, challenging her to argue.

They knew each other too well. Yeah, she probably would have spat in his glass.

She mouthed the words. *You. Are. So. Dead.*

The jerk just grinned before ignoring her and turning to discuss who should go first with Jason.

The game went on for nearly two hours, at which point Nicole was fighting to keep from straight-out yawning in their faces. She'd gone bankrupt a good forty-five minutes earlier.

The guys continued their cutthroat game, seemingly oblivious to her increasing ants in the pants.

"Ha!" Jason howled with delight. Troy's final roll landed him on Jason's most expensive lot. He thrust his fists in the air, roaring as if there were a crowd cheering in the distance before returning to position and offering a cocky grin. "And that, my friends, is how the game is played."

Troy handed the last of his money across the board with a good-natured grin. "You got me. Well done."

"And that was so much fun," Nicole announced, perkiness dripping from every word.

Troy's lips twitched, but Jason seemed to miss her sarcasm. "We'll have to do it again sometime," he suggested.

Right after my lobotomy, Nicole thought as she gathered up empty snack bowls and glasses and carried them into the kitchen, shoving everything into the dishwasher as she fought to regain her sense of humour.

It took a while.

By the time she got back, the guys had the game put away and were standing by the door, deep in discussion. The Monopoly box was tucked under Jason's arm, his coat draped over it.

"I don't think they got the timing belt quite right," Jason complained.

"Bring it by tomorrow," Troy offered, looking thoughtful for a moment. "After lunch. I should have time to look at it."

Jason smacked a hand on his shoulder before turning to Nicole. "Thanks for an awesome evening. It was great."

She stepped closer, waiting for Troy to leave so she

could at least finish the date somewhat normally. A goodbye kiss would be better than nothing at all.

Troy didn't budge. Just stood there, smiling innocently as if he didn't know damn well that she wanted his ass out of the house.

"Awesome night, as always," he said to Nic before bumping her date with a closed fist. "Oh, hey, Jason. You mentioned you were thinking about learning to fish." He tilted his head toward the street. "I got my new rod and reel in the truck. Wanna see?"

"Definitely." Jason followed him to the door, glancing over his shoulder with a final smile for Nicole. "Thanks, again. Great evening. I guess I'll see you at the office."

The jerks left.

She included both of them in that description because now Jason was in her bad books as well as Troy. She managed to wait until the door was closed and the guys were well away, standing by the tailgate of Troy's truck. Then the words burst free.

"Son of a *bitch*."

She wasn't sure which of them she was yelling at.

A truly impressive jumble of frustration wrapped around her. Boredom mixed with the sexual tension Troy had flash-fire started and then let fizzle away, and...

What the freak had just happened?

CHAPTER 2

Troy drove off right after Jason did, turning at the first corner and doubling back. He slipped into the parking spot behind Nicole's place.

Time to find out what the hell was going on.

He stomped up the back stairs and yanked open the door. "Nic?"

No answer.

He glanced around the kitchen before pacing into the living room. Empty—she'd vanished.

"Nic," he shouted louder as he headed toward the back of the house and her bedroom.

No wonder she hadn't answered. A faint light escaped from the bathroom where the shower was blasting at full volume. He marched forward, pausing at the door.

The clear shower curtain allowed enough light to shine through that her body was nicely showcased from top to bottom. He folded his arms and watched in appreciation as she rinsed the shampoo out of her hair, bubbles slipping over her face and down her curves. Her hands danced over her skin, just the places he'd like to be touching, and Troy eased his position to relieve some of the pressure on his rising cock.

Cool as a cucumber, without even looking his direction, she gave him shit. "Are you going to stand there all night gawking, or you are going to tell me what the hell you were thinking, coming over here and messing up my date?"

Troy chuckled. "I like how you don't even blink to find me in your bathroom."

She stepped to the edge of the bath, jerking the shower curtain back a few inches so she could glare at him more easily, water dripping down her face, her bangs hanging in her eyes. "I knew you'd show up. Kind of expected you to wait till Jason drove off and then march right back so you could annoy me faster. *Jerk.*"

"I figured I should give at least the appearance of leaving." Troy admired the view, his gaze lingering on her breasts. "What're you so pissed off about? I had no idea some random guy was going to be here."

"Bullshit." Nic cut the water, shoving back the shower curtain with a strong sweep of her arm. She shoved her hand forward in a clear demand.

"No shit," he insisted, grabbing the towel from beside his shoulder and shaking it out. Instead of stuffing it into her hand, he reached forward and draped it around her body, picking her up and placing her on the bathmat. "As far as I knew, we were on for the evening like usual."

Nicole shrugged out of his grasp, escaping into her bedroom where she rubbed the towel vigorously over tempting, wet skin. "Good lord, Troy, don't make me go through all this again. I sent you an email and explained everything. It's been fun, but it's time to move to the next thing, which means I need to date. So don't stop by to hook up anymore, *yada yada yada...*"

Troy settled on her bed, confused as all get out. Watching her hadn't made his aching cock any easier to ignore. And it didn't help when, without a lick of embarrassment, she dropped the towel to the floor and reached into her dresser.

He dragged his gaze off her bare ass. "Well, that would have made a difference. *If* I'd gotten your email, but since I didn't, I still don't know what you're talking about."

She jerked a T-shirt over her head—one of his that she'd stolen at some point—then reached for her phone. "You're so annoying. Fine. I'll show you proof."

She flipped through the screens then passed it over triumphantly.

He read through the message. "It's been fun... Need to date... No more Netflix and chill..." Troy glanced up. "Number one, I've never seen this before in my life. You didn't send it to me."

"I know I did," she insisted.

"Nope." He shook his head. "I hope you didn't send it to one of my brothers."

Her eyes widened. "*Fuck*, I hope not."

"Or my dad," Troy deadpanned. "That would make things real awkward the next time—"

"Shut. Up." She snatched the phone from him and checked frantically. "Oh my God, okay. It's still in drafts. I guess I forgot to hit send."

"Apology accepted." Troy leaned back and blinked, offering his most innocent expression.

"Screw you."

"And number two," he continued as if she hadn't spoken, "I still don't get it, this sudden urge to 'date'. What does that even mean? You have some weird compulsion to be bored to tears? I mean, I can totally understand how hot you must have been for Jason. The dude was super-enticing, with that steamy move preempting Ventnor Avenue and all."

"*God.*"

She plopped onto the bed beside him, flinging her arms and legs out as her head hit the pillow with a thud. He held his amusement. Melodrama wasn't usually her thing, but the flounce fit.

"What's up, Nic?" he asked seriously.

"It's...complicated."

Troy stretched beside her, years of familiarity between them easing the awkwardness. "Not usually. Unless you've decided to turn your love of unsolvable puzzles on your sex life, just to mix it up."

"This isn't about sex," she insisted, a low unhappy sound following hard on the heels of the comment. "Dammit to hell, it *can't* be about sex. If it were about sex then you and me would be bouncing the mattress right now, fucking our brains out."

"No prob..."

Troy rolled her under him, taking her lips and kissing her decisively. She'd sounded so confused and sad it seemed only right to give her something else to think about. Or not think about.

A good, hard tumble should do it.

Warm, soft curves filled his hands as he skimmed his palms up the sides of her body, their lips and tongues tangling enthusiastically.

She was on board at the start, wrapping her legs around his hips. Digging her fingers into his shoulders. Kissing him back hungrily.

Then her new agenda must have intervened. "We're not supposed to do this. No more booty calls," Nic murmured against his mouth even as she reached between their bodies, fighting to undo his top button. "I need to move on."

Her lips skated over his jaw, then her teeth nipped his chin the instant before she moaned. Her hips rose as she rubbed against the hard length of his cock.

"Move on to what? *God*, Nic, that feels so fucking good."

"Hmmm, yes, right there." A low, needy sigh escaped her followed by a curse. "Dammit, Troy. We can't do this."

"We can." He dipped his head and put his teeth to the hard point of her nipple, biting lightly through the thin cotton T-shirt. "We are."

Another needy groan, but this time she let go of his shoulders, sliding her hands to his chest and pushing him away instead of holding him close. "Please. Help me stop..."

Troy rolled away, body throbbing with the need to continue, but he knew better than to keep going after a woman said *stop*. He stared at the ceiling for a moment and fought to steady his breathing, thinking of icy-cold things. Picturing the most boring engine tune-up ever to wipe away images of Nic naked, riding his cock.

It took a few minutes before he could speak without groaning in frustration. "It's complicated?" he repeated.

"Yeah."

"I have time to listen," he offered, rolling to his side and staring at her flushed face. A chuckle escaped. "It's not as if we're doing anything else interesting at the moment."

Nic crawled backward until she was propped against the headboard. "I..." She made a face. "This is super awkward."

"More awkward than discovering we had sex too close to the motion sensor at the wetland reserve, and now there're pictures of my ass floating around the forestry-service back rooms?"

She laughed. "That will only be awkward if anyone ever IDs your ass."

"Which we both know will happen at the most inopportune moment possible." Troy snickered. "I should run for mayor."

Another burst of laughter escaped her, and something warmed inside. Maybe they weren't fucking around like he'd hoped, but he'd still pulled her from her funky mood. He'd take any win he could, especially if it meant she was smiling instead of frustrated and upset.

NICOLE STROKED a finger over his cheek, thankful he'd decided to be reasonable. "Okay, so here's the thing. Cyndi's expecting."

He waited in silence for a moment before shaking his head. "If that was a clue, it wasn't enough," he said. "Congrats to her and Kevin, but I don't know why your sister getting pregnant means *we're* not having sex."

Oops. Yeah, she'd missed a good half-dozen steps in there. "Sorry. It's like...a chain reaction happened all of a sudden in my brain. Cyndi and Kevin already have two kids. Jodie and Dale have three, so I don't know if they're even going to have anymore, although they did mention four was possible. So if I want to have kids that are—"

"You want to have *kids*?" he interrupted, jerking upright to stare at her in shock. "Since when?"

"That's what I'm explaining," she said, the irritation in her tone noticeable even to herself. She took a deep breath and started over, more rational and calm. "Yes, I want to have babies. I've always been thinking 'someday I'll have a family', but I've realized if I want to have kids that are around the same age as their cousins, I need to get rolling. Which means no more fucking around with you."

"And it's vital to base your baby production on when your sisters are popping out kids?" A frown creased his forehead. "Nope. Don't get it."

As confused as he sounded, he wasn't being an ass, so Nicole tried again. "Family is important. I've always planned on having at least a couple kids. And yes, I want my kids to have cousins near the same age they can be friends with, so if I don't want to miss out before my sisters hang up the baby-making gear, I need to move on to the next thing."

"Mike's not having kids yet," Troy pointed out.

She made a face. "He's not a kid person. He'll probably have kids only because his wife wants them, *if* he gets married, which who knows how many eons from now that will be. I'm not holding my breath and waiting for either miracle to occur."

Troy batted his fingers against his thigh, the way he did when he was thinking hard. Or annoyed. "You want to have kids, so you need to date."

"Well, I'd kind of like to have them the old-fashioned way, yeah," she said. "Which means I need to find a guy to have them with. Which means dating."

"What? You don't think they've come up with a Studs R Us app for baby-making yet? Swipe right for 'impregnate me now'?"

She smacked him lightly on the arm. "Stop it. I'm not going to grab some random guy, you know. I'm also looking for someone I enjoy spending time with. Someone I want to be with forever."

"Awesome."

His entire attitude had grown unreadable. Nicole twisted to a sitting position to face him. "What's wrong?"

Troy shook his head. "Nothing."

Only he was on the edge of the bed now, straightening his clothes and grabbing his shoes from the floor.

Nicole watched as he put them on. "Are you mad at me?"

He made a noncommittal noise that could be a no. Or a yes. Or the result of a bad taco for supper.

She crawled closer and laid a hand on his arm. "You knew things weren't serious between us."

His fingers closed over hers, and he squeezed briefly before pulling himself free and rising to his feet. His devilish smile was back in place, eyes flashing as if he didn't have a care in the world. "Of course I knew we weren't serious. You just threw me for a loop, sweetheart. That's a big change you've got going on, but if it's what you want, no prob. I should get out of your hair and let you make plans, or whatever you need to do."

"Sleep?" Nicole teased. "Since it's late?"

"Right." Troy nodded once then turned on his heel and marched from the room.

The temperature seemed to drop ten degrees when he left, and she sat back and stared at the empty doorframe, listening as his footsteps faded into the distance. The back-door opened and closed firmly—but not firmly enough to be slammed shut.

He'd been reasonable. Understanding, really, yet...

It wasn't as if she'd expected a goodbye kiss after sharing her decision, but his total lack of reaction left her feeling uncomfortable and disjointed.

If he'd ranted and called her a fool, it would have hurt.

Or if he'd laughed and called her an idiot, it would have offended her, but either way she could've gotten blazing mad at him for daring to judge her.

Instead he'd pulled the wind from her sails and neither agreed with her, nor fought her, and she felt...

Felt...

Empty.

As if a piece of her wasn't sitting in the right order anymore.

She should have expected it, though. Moving on affected both of them, and changes sucked.

But her sisters had gone from being wild party girls to finding great guys they'd fallen madly in love with. Guys who were now solid, dependable husbands and proud daddies of the families they were raising.

It was time for Nicole to step in a new direction, and that meant away from Troy Thompson. That was all.

But if her decision was that simple, she should have rolled over and gone to sleep. Instead, she found herself rushing into the kitchen a moment later, staring out the window at Troy's monster truck as he backed into the alley. He glanced toward her, the yard light shining off his impenetrable expression before he focused away from her and drove off.

She wondered where he was going...

...and the fact she wondered at all annoyed her even more than his earlier lack of response.

CHAPTER 3

Astiff drink. That's what he needed. Maybe a double, and keep them coming. Liquor easing down his throat until he was numb and the conversation he'd just had was nothing but a blurred memory. Perfect. He'd go get a bottle and finish it off...

Except since he didn't fucking *drink*, getting shit-faced oblivious was out of the bloody question.

He could go find a fight. Dangerous and violent. Fists and pain and a whole lot of shouting voices, loud enough to drown out the roaring in his ears.

Nicole Adams wanted babies.

Oh, right, and a guy to go with them. A guy who was *not* Troy, so *thanks very much for all the fun fucking around we've had, but I need to move on to some perfectly boring asshole with willing sperm.*

Suddenly Monopoly Man was so much more explainable. Jason must be considered a good donor candidate. Dude had a respectable job that paid well. Decent looking—heck, Troy wondered if Nic had done a genetic background check on the ass.

He turned so sharply at the next corner tires squealed and rubber burned.

To hell with going home yet. Mike was there with Tessa, and while there was no longer any reason to not join in for a threesome, he had zero desire to go that route. Not tonight.

Tonight he wanted to burn off steam, and he wasn't even sure he could put a name to exactly *why* he was so fucking pissed off. He'd known the relationship was short term. He'd goddamn *known* at some point she'd say she'd had enough, but...

He jerked the wheel to the left and headed to his oldest brother's place.

Since he wasn't going to drink, fight *or* fuck, he might as well annoy the hell out of his family. Dropping in on Clay and Maggie would distract him from his foul mood nicely. He needed some mothering tonight.

He usually let his oldest brother do that.

Amusement snuck past his brewing discontent as he knocked on their back door. It was barely after ten. Maybe he could sweet talk Maggie into letting him raid their fridge.

Only, no one answered, not for the longest time. Troy was on the verge of walking in like he had at Nic's when the door finally moved.

Clay wore nothing but a pair of sweatpants, low on his hips, and his expression was far from welcoming.

"Who's dead?" his brother demanded.

Troy considered. "No one."

"Anyone dying? Bleeding out?"

"Nope." Troy folded his arms over his chest. "You're in a gory state of mind."

"Good night, Troy."

Clay pushed the door, and it swung toward Troy. He

shot out a hand to stop it before it could close entirely. "*Hey*. What the hell?"

His brother glared harder. "Go home."

"But I thought—"

His words ground to a halt as he finally clued in. The yellow glow in the barely visible living room was caused by candlelight, and soft music played in the background. As tempting as it was to stand there and continue to annoy Clay, he liked Maggie too much to massacre the romantic evening he'd interrupted.

He backed away. "Sorry. I'll see you at the shop on Monday."

"Troy, wait." Clay's expression softened. "You okay?" he asked. "I mean, you've got shitty timing, but I'm not about to kick you to the curb if something's wrong."

"I'm fine." Troy waved a hand. "Get back to what you're doing."

Clay didn't bother to answer, just grinned as he closed the door and left Troy standing there.

Another rush of gut-twisting emotion tangled through him. So. Not only was he cut off from sex, he was cut off and his big brother was scoring.

Something was not right in the world.

Ten minutes later it was clear Fate was truly enjoying herself and having a good hard laugh at his expense. He pulled into the driveway at Mitch and Anna's, dimming his headlights as he eyeballed the living room, not wanting to interrupt *another* date night at home.

There were no candles involved this time, at least. Troy jogged around the side of the house, jerking to a stop when he heard angry voices through the open living room window.

"You're not being logical," Mitch snapped.

"And you're being a bossy bastard," Anna retorted. "Like usual."

"You like it when I'm bossy. Besides, I'm right, and you damn well know it."

Troy backed away rapidly. He didn't want to get in the middle of any fight, although he was disappointed to discover the two of them—

Something crashed, followed by a loud thump, and warning bells went off like crazy. Screw not getting involved in his brother's affairs. Something was wrong. Troy ran toward the window...

For fuck's sake.

Whatever they'd been arguing about was either forgotten or some screwed-up version of foreplay. Mitch had Anna up against the wall, and the two of them were kissing like fiends, clothes falling away in the split second before Troy turned his back and escaped.

He wasn't even going to attempt his little sister's place, because if Katy wasn't making out with Gage, they'd be up with his year-old nephew, Tanner. He loved the kid, but no way in hell he was going anywhere near a rugrat tonight.

He hesitated before heading to Len and Janey's then decided to take the risk. By now his inexplicable anger had cooled, but he was still hoping for a dose of family.

A slow drive past their backyard kept his tires rolling. His middle brother sat by the fire pit in their backyard, Janey in his lap, the two of them cuddled up and kissing.

Was everyone in the frickin' world fooling around tonight except *him?*

Troy drove to the Thompson and Sons garage. He pulled on a coverall and headed to the first job lined up for the following morning. He wasn't scheduled to work until

Monday—Clay and Mitch were covering the weekend—but he might as well do something productive while he stewed.

He was lying on a mechanics creeper, slipping under the car to access the oil pan, when the lights by the far wall clicked on.

"Who's there?" a deep, masculine voice demanded.

Troy rolled out and sat up to spot his dad stepping cautiously down the stairs.

"Over here. It's—" He swore and dropped behind the hood of the car as his dad swung a shotgun toward him. "Jesus, Dad, put that damn thing away," he shouted. "It's Troy."

Keith Thompson muttered under his breath, then stomped across the floor to the nearest workbench, laying the shotgun on the surface. "Damn *fool*. What're you doing here so late, sneaking around in the dark?"

"An oil change," Troy snapped.

"You can't find anything better to do at this hour?" his dad demanded.

"No." He was too pissed off to even attempt an excuse. "What the hell is wrong with you? Pulling a gun on me. You could hurt someone with that shit."

Keith gazed at him for a moment before his face twitched. "That's kind of the idea of a shotgun, you know. To shoot things."

"*Don't* fucking joke about this. Even if we have a freaking break-in, don't you *ever* bring a gun in here again." Troy stared his father down from a good extra four inches of height. "Let them steal everything in the goddamn shop if they want."

His dad straightened, anger rising in his eyes. "Watch your language and don't boss me around."

"Well, someone has to, since you've obviously taken leave of your senses."

"Of all my children, you're the last one who gets to lecture me. You're still wet behind the ears." His dad turned his back and stomped away, shouting over his shoulder. "Want a drink?"

As if Keith hadn't just threatened to shoot Troy then insulted him on top of it.

Troy dragged a hand through his hair and counted to ten. "No thanks," he gritted through his teeth.

Keith disappeared into the staff area, but he was back a moment later, popping the top on a beer then offering it to Troy.

Troy shook his head. "No."

His dad shrugged then took a drink, leaning back on the nearest bench, making himself comfortable. "Still don't know what you're doing here."

Since Troy didn't know himself, it wasn't as if he had a ready answer. "Just needed to burn off some energy."

Keith chuckled. "You usually think of a better way to work it off than fighting with dirty oil pans. Getting into trouble, breaking hearts and all that."

Troy stared firmly at the tool chest in front of him and worked to keep a positive mind-set instead of snapping back at his father. "Yeah, well, not tonight."

"You coming down with something?" his dad asked, concern staining his voice. "Never known you to pick work over play."

Fuck it all. Troy knew he shouldn't ask. Knew it the instant the words hit his tongue, but it seemed tonight he was a glutton for punishment.

"What're you saying? That I'm a slacker?"

"'Course not. I mean, not really. You're young, having

fun, sowing oats. The usual. You always have a good time. It's what you do."

And...that quickly, he'd had enough. Troy didn't think he could keep a civil tongue in his head for much longer. "Gotta go. I'll see you on Monday."

He peeled off his overalls and tossed them over the nearest horizontal surface he could find before striding for the door. The fists he held clenched by his sides were shaking, he was so upset.

Pissed off again, but at least this time he knew why. What was that, three times in one night? Seems he was going for a new record.

Behind him, his dad laughed softly. "Always jumping from one thing to the next. Stay out of trouble, son. We'll see you 'round."

Troy slammed the truck door and fought to even his breathing. He would not race out of the lot like a speed demon and give his father a chance to mock him on Monday.

Then again, maybe Keith wouldn't even notice, like he'd *never* fucking noticed that Troy didn't drink. Not ever.

There were an awful lot of other things his father, and his siblings, had never noticed, because that was how Troy had wanted it, but tonight for some reason the secrets he was holding, and his lack of connection to them all *burned*.

He loved them. His family was his fucking *everything*, but sometimes he wanted to take the lot of them, sit them down, and make them open their bloody eyes and *see*.

And yet...them knowing his secrets was the exact opposite of what he'd always worked for, and the dilemma just made his blood boil and his brain ache.

What a shitty day.

"CAN I GET A FAVOUR?"

Nicole blinked as she changed her focus from the computer screen to the office receptionist. "What's up?"

"I know Mondays you usually take a late lunch, but can you go now then mind the desk while I'm gone?" Kerry asked. "I have to head out, and I need someone to deal with drop-ins."

Nicole glanced at her watch. A change of timing was no big deal. She saved her project then grabbed her purse. "Sure. I'll be back as quick as I can."

"Don't rush." Kerry pointed toward the partners who stood in a group by the coffee machine. "They're heading into a meeting for the next hour, and I can't leave until they're done."

Nicole glanced over, and Jason caught her eye. He offered a smile, but he hadn't done more than simply say hello that morning. He must've been just as impressed with their Friday evening as she was.

She headed outdoors, thinking hard about the wisdom of dating someone where she worked. Not that she was jumping up and down to spend more time with the man. He was nice enough, she supposed, but there hadn't been any sparks.

That's because Troy burned through all the kindling, her brain taunted.

Nicole pushed through the doors of the café, telling her brain to kindly shut up.

The place was a madhouse. This was why she didn't usually go for lunch at five minutes after twelve. There didn't seem to be an empty chair anywhere. Nicole rotated slowly, debating if she should give up and settle for the granola bar she kept in her desk.

Her gaze met a pair of cool blue eyes and a welcoming smile set in a somewhat familiar face. The blonde patted the back of the empty seat next to her where she was tucked in the corner at a small table.

Nicole made her way across the floor, scrambling through her memories. The woman was familiar, but her name hovered on the tip of Nicole's tongue. They must have gone to school together, but the blonde had to be at least a few years younger, so they wouldn't have shared any classes.

Recall of the woman's name and particulars arrived the moment Nicole reached the table, and there was no time to abandon ship without being really rude.

Her mystery woman had risen to her feet and was holding out a hand in welcome. "Laurel Sitko," she offered as a reminder. "The place is packed, but I don't mind if you join me."

It wasn't who she'd expected to share a meal with, but Nicole supposed she was safe enough. It's not as if the pastor's daughter was going to haul her over to the dark side in a mere thirty minutes.

"Where did all these people come from?" Nicole settled in the chair beside Laurel's.

"Tour bus? I'm not sure." Laurel wrinkled her nose as she gazed around the room. "I thought I knew everybody in Rocky, but I've been gone for three years. It's possible some of them live here now."

"Easy enough to tell," Nicole grumbled. "Is there anyone under the age of forty, male, and moderately attractive? If so, they have to be visiting."

Laurel laughed, a bright, light sound that brought smiles

to the people at the tables next to them. Nicole found her lips twitching involuntarily as well.

Then Laurel leaned closer, whispering just loud enough for Nicole to hear, "We need to set up the modern equivalent of mail-order brides, only with sexy, eligible bachelors. They don't even need to have jobs, as long as they're *very* good with their hands."

Nicole attempted to swallow the mouthful she'd just sipped from her water glass, but it was no use. Moisture dribbled down her chin, and she wiped at her face and choked for air as Laurel patted her soothingly on the shoulder.

When she could finally breathe, she gave Laurel a far more thorough once-over. "Am I mixed up?" she asked. "Am I confusing you with someone else?"

Laurel's eyes sparkled. "Excuse me?"

"Pastor's daughter? Class valedictorian?"

"Don't forget the new label. Librarian technician." The young woman nodded. "None of which are required to have *stick in the mud* in the definition the last time I checked, in case that's what you were thinking."

She was a smart cookie. Nicole's smile widened. "Good to know."

One of the harried café waitresses scurried up, took their orders then vanished in a whirlwind. Nicole glanced around, more for a chance to think than because she was curious about the customers in the cafe.

Laurel *was* younger than her, and definitely not a part of the crowd Nicole was used to hanging out with. Yet, considering all the changes she had planned, making a new friend who was a little less the wild party animal was probably a good thing.

She turned back to her seatmate. "Librarian?"

"Technician," Laurel emphasized. "I've only completed two years so far, but it's enough to qualify for a practicum position."

"You'll be around for the summer?"

"Longer than that, depending on what happens at the library."

Nicole nodded. "Are you living back at home?"

Laurel shuddered before looking sheepish. "Definitely not. I found a one-bedroom to rent. I wanted to come back to Rocky, but that *doesn't* mean I want to go back to being under my parents' roof."

"I hear you." Nicole patted Laurel sympathetically on the hand. "I felt the same way last year when I finished school. All my family is here, and I think I want to stay, but I'm not twelve anymore."

"Tell me it gets easier," Laurel begged earnestly. "I'm still getting the *you know your old bedroom is open* suggestion every time I visit them, and I'm ready to scream."

"Just think how much you'd save if you lived at home," Nicole deadpanned. "You don't need to deal with all that yard work. Are you stopping by for dinner tonight?"

Laurel groaned, hanging her head in her hands.

Nicole laughed softly. "Buck up. I guess that means they love us."

The other woman nodded, a wistful expression in her eyes. "They could love us from a distance, couldn't they? That would be far more convenient."

They exchanged another laugh before the conversation dove off into books they liked, and music, and by the time their meals were just about done, Nicole was pretty sure she'd found a new BFF.

It was a little shocking to discover since Laurel was one

of the last people she would've imagined to have been a kindred spirit.

"Nic, *baby*. You're a sight for sore eyes."

Nicole glanced up to discover one of her guy friends standing over the table, another man at his side. "Glenn. Hey, it's been a long time."

"Ages. At least a month or two." He offered a wink before tilting his head to indicate his buddy. "Meet Darrell. Cousin of mine. He's thinking about moving to Rocky."

Miracles would never cease. Under the age of forty, male, and moderately attractive. Maybe Laurel was giving off heavenly vibes and prayers were being answered.

"Nice to meet you," Nicole said with complete honesty.

Darrell nodded, meeting her eyes for just a moment before glancing away.

Shy, or extremely shy, one of the two.

Glenn more than made up for his cousin. "He's an accountant. Business stuff, kind of like you, only he works for himself."

Nicole tried to catch Darrell's gaze. "That's great."

"Yeah, he's obsessive about numbers. Fits him to a T." Glenn elbowed his cousin in the side. "Anyway, there's a party happening Friday night at the Blackstones'. Wondered if you're going."

Maybe Nicole should take it as a good sign that she hadn't even known about the house party. Maybe she was already becoming grownup, responsible and respectable.

Boring. Boring and *no sex,* her brain shouted.

Shut up, she told her brain.

Before she could answer, Darrell shifted uncomfortably then offered a timid smile. "If you don't have a date yet, I'd love to go with you."

Awwww. How sweet. The party hadn't tempted her,

but his invitation was more in line with her current requirements, and the setting would be a safe place to get to know someone new.

"Sounds like fun. I'd love to." She offered a wide smile, and Darrell's eyes lit up, before he looked away. "You want to meet there?" Nicole asked.

Darrell nodded wordlessly.

Nicole turned to Laurel. "You going?"

Laurel blinked hard, shock on her face as if Nicole had just asked if the other woman wanted to strip naked and dance on the table. "Going *where*?"

The guys seemed to notice Laurel for the first time.

"Oh. Sure, whatever. You're welcome to come too, I guess," Glenn offered, although he didn't seem very excited about it.

"Thanks so much." Laurel's lips twitched. "It sounds *peachy*."

Nicole stopped from snorting. Just.

"Awesome. Eight o'clock then." Without waiting for a response, Glenn flicked his fingers in a mock salute then bumped his shoulder into his cousin. "Let's go."

Nicole watched until they left the café, feeling a little as if she'd entered the Twilight Zone. "That was weird."

She glanced over at Laurel who was primly eating the last of her french fries, staring out the window with amusement in her eyes.

"What's so funny?" Nicole asked. "And please don't say *'Golly gee,* I don't know what you're talking about', because I'll hurl."

Laurel snickered. "Don't worry, your lunch is safe."

"So...?"

"I'm thinking how much fun I can have freaking people out. I'll wear white, and wander around with my hands like this…" she clasped them together as if she were praying "…and every chance I get I'll open back rooms and wander in on people—"

"You're evil," Nicole said with a grin. "Truly *inspiringly* evil."

"Thank you, I try." Laurel fluttered her lashes, looking as if butter wouldn't melt in her mouth. That lasted for all of ten seconds before her smile widened. "I have to say this has been one of the most entertaining lunch breaks I've had in a long time. Thank you for sharing my table, Nicole Adams."

"Thanks for not being a stick in the mud," Nicole tossed back.

They made arrangements for Friday evening before heading back to work, Nicole pondering the results of her incredibly productive lunch hour.

A new friend. Maybe this changing to be a better, more responsible person was going to work out all right, if it meant having people like Laurel join her life.

Oh, *and* she had a date. Hurrah.

Her sheer lack of enthusiasm at the idea of spending time with Darrell was frustrating. She needed to get her head back into the game, and soon. It wasn't his fault he wasn't Tr—

Alert. Alert. Here be monsters.

No, that line of thinking was not where she needed to go. Darrell might be a *wonderful* date. They'd have a great time, and maybe they'd hit it off, and even if they didn't it was good for her to spend time with her new attitude.

Everything now needed to move toward having a family of her own. It was a *damn* worthwhile goal, and she was going to do everything she could to reach it.

Bor—

Shut up, brain, she ordered before the thought had fully formed.

She rolled her eyes at herself then started plotting for the party.

She was going to have a good time if it killed her. And thoughts of the fun she could be having with Troy would *not* interfere.

CHAPTER 4

Troy hated the new guy on sight.

He wasn't in the most receptive mood in the first place. He wasn't over his mad from the previous Friday. Plus, Troy had spent the weekend avoiding his family, and all this week he'd been ducking out of the apartment as fast as he could because no way did he want to accidentally get drawn into a discussion with Mike about how stupid his sister was behaving.

So even now, a few days later, he was predisposed to dislike whoever Nic hauled out as a better, upgraded model, but he hadn't thought he'd be confronted with a second jackass a week after the first.

Seemed she was serious about this settling-down bullshit.

Then again, this wasn't the setting he'd expected to find her looking for a baby daddy. The Blackstones were known for their loud and crazy house parties, and Troy had figured it was a safe place to work out his frustrations over all the crap that had set him on edge.

Strolling through the dancing bodies in the living room

had been fine, as had the short break discussing sports with some of his buddies in the area outside the dining room.

He continued to wander and visit, sauntering around the corner to where a dozen or so people were gathered more quietly. They'd grabbed lawn chairs and were using coolers for side tables. Chatting and flirting and hanging out.

He was drawn like a magnet to the middle where Nic sat, her dark hair swinging in an arc as she twisted to laugh at something the guy beside her said. She wore deep-red lipstick, and Troy couldn't peel his gaze from her mouth. Mesmerized, drawn forward...

Until it registered he didn't recognize the guy she was talking to.

Troy's spine stiffened as he looked the other man over. Seemed safe enough. Dark haired, lean, but not lean enough to be considered scrawny. He seemed to have trouble looking Nic in the eyes, though, and Troy observed silently for a while, trying to figure out what bugged him the most about the whole situation.

A hand landed on his shoulder, a firm grip squeezing for a brief second. "Nice to see you're still in the land of the living."

Troy glanced sideways to discover his roommate. "Hey."

Mike grinned. "You've been making yourself scarce lately. I didn't even hear you come in last night."

Troy wasn't about to confess he'd deliberately stayed away until Mike's lady visitor had left. "You've been seeing a lot of Tessa lately. Having a good time?"

"As always. She's working tonight, though. Might drop by after her shift." Mike's gaze drifted over the party, his smile fading as he spotted his twin. "Dude. Who's the guy beside Nic?"

"Don't know." Which should have been followed by the words *don't care*, but Troy couldn't bring himself to outright lie.

Mike's lips twisted into an evil grin. "Well, then. Since it's my place to be a loving and protective big brother, I'd better go find out."

He sauntered across the distance, coming to a stop in front of his sister. Troy folded his arms, amusement rising as he waited for the fireworks to begin.

Nic glanced his way, her eyes narrowing as her gaze darted between him and her brother before she offered him a truly wicked glare.

Troy shrugged as if to say it wasn't his fault, then he casually slid closer as he pretended to join a conversation a few feet to their right.

Made it easier to eavesdrop.

"You're an accountant. Oh." Mike considered before nodding. "Guess we could always use another one of those in town."

"If you know anyone who needs help, I'd appreciate an introduction," the guy said, his voice barely audible.

Troy attempted to step closer without *looking* as if he was stepping closer.

Mike wasn't nearly done. "So, Darrell, you staying with Glenn?"

"Until I figure out if I'm sticking around."

"You might not stick around? Think there's something wrong with Rocky?" Mike demanded.

"No, but—"

"It might not be for everyone, but we're damn proud of living here."

"I'm sure, and I didn't mean—"

Troy glanced over his shoulder. Nic was squeezing her

lips together as her brother continued to grill Darrell. Clearly she wasn't enjoying the interruption but couldn't figure out how to make it stop without resorting to her usual method of telling Mike to fuck off and die.

Which probably didn't fit her new, more serious persona.

The evening was improving by the minute.

"Let me get those drinks we talked about." Nic rose. "See you in a minute or two."

"Take your time." Mike settled into her empty chair, looking as if he had no intention of stopping his rapid-fire questions for the next hour or so.

The other man looked thoroughly uncomfortable.

Troy forgave his best friend for all past sins then followed Nicole into the surprisingly empty kitchen.

She pulled a couple beers out of the ice bucket on the counter before turning toward him. Her eyes widened. She opened her mouth then slammed it shut.

He grinned. Didn't say anything, just *grinned*.

Her glare returned. The deadly one he enjoyed so much.

"Troy." Icy cold and controlled. Tight, like a rock shot from a sling.

"*Nicole.*" He lowered his voice and made it sound as if they were in the bedroom, one step away from him sinking into her heat.

"Troy." She glanced around before fisting her hands on her hips. "Stop that."

He chuckled. "Are you sure?"

Her breathing grew heavier, rising anger bringing a rosy flush to her cheeks. Her cherry-red lips curled into a pout. "Do you *mind*? I'm on a *date*."

Troy laid a hand over his chest. "Really?"

"Don't be a jerk."

"I'm not." He hesitated then offered a sheepish smile. "Okay, I'm totally being one, but are you serious? That's the best you can do?"

"He's...sweet."

For fuck's sake. His amusement faded and that lingering annoyance was back with a vengeance. "You hate sweet. You chew up sweet and spit it out like year-old Peeps you found in the back of the cupboard."

"You're so annoying," she muttered.

"You're making my brain hurt, Nic," he drawled. "You want to date, I get that. But I thought you wanted kids. I don't understand why you're not looking for guys who have testosterone in their system. Did he slip something in your drink that shorted your brain?"

"Some guys are intellectually exciting," Nic insisted. She turned her back on him, pausing to pour one beer into a glass.

"God, *seriously?* That's for the loser, isn't it?"

"Darrell said he likes the way a good beer tastes out of a glass."

"Seriously? Even *I* know that's nothing like a good beer."

She bit down on her lip, but he still noticed her snicker.

Only she pulled herself together then calmly ordered him to take a hike. "Go away, Troy."

He hated seeing her like this. Hated how fake it all seemed, and how absolutely bored to tears she was.

This wasn't Nic, and suddenly that was the breaking point. If she'd been having a good time, maybe he would have backed off, but he'd be damned if he'd watch her bury her energy and enthusiasm in some mistaken variation of Dr. Jekyll and Mr. Hyde.

She needed a *Come to Jesus* moment, and Troy looked forward to preaching to her very much.

IT WAS TOO much to hope that Troy's momentary silence meant he was going to listen to her and get out of her face.

Instead, he stepped behind her, hands landing on the counter on either side of her hips. Trapping her in place as he whispered in her ear, "Intellectually exciting. Really. Is that how he's going to get you off later? Reading you his latest financial reports?"

The big brute stood close enough that heat traveled between them, their hips brushing. Every inch of her completely aware of every inch of him surrounding her.

"I'm very interested in solid financial numbers," she said as primly as possible.

"I'll give you a solid number," he offered as their hips bumped again. "Nine solid inches."

Good grief. Heat rushed through her, the challenge too much to resist. Nicole turned on the spot, falling into his eyes for a moment before remembering she needed to stay focused. "You don't want to get into a dick war with me," she whispered. "I have a whole *drawer* full of dicks, and they're all bigger than yours."

He opened his mouth again, but whatever he was about to say stuttered to a stop as she lowered a hand and deliberately pressed it over the front of his jeans.

Troy swallowed hard, hips rocking into her as if he had no control over the impulse.

A shiver rippled over her entire body. Nine inches was a low estimate. She knew from personal, intimate detail he was a handful and a half.

They stood there, in the middle of the kitchen, sexual tension rising by the second. Her date was waiting to be rescued from her evil, cruel brother. People could wander in at any second, and still the most urgent need rushing her was the desire to rip open Troy's zipper, reach in and pull out his cock.

Maybe drop to her knees and...

Not happening. *Not* happening.

Damn, but she wanted it to.

Troy leaned against her, the front of their bodies touching as his lips brushed her ear. "Come with me."

The words were clearly an order, and she shivered again. "*Troy.*"

"Troy, *yes?*"

He didn't wait for an answer. He caught her by the hand, pulling her out of the kitchen and down a short side hallway. He jerked open the nearest door and guided her into the dark space ahead of him, one big hand a brand on her lower back.

The scent of cleaners hit her the same instant she spotted mops and cleaning supplies in the meager light from the hall, then the door was closed and she was being pressed against the back of it.

All around them was utterly dark and infinitely dangerous as Troy lined up his rock-solid body against her, taking command of her lips and kissing her as if he were starving.

A week ago he'd had her in this position, and here they were again, but this time she wasn't going to stop him.

She needed this, and only Troy could ease the craving.

He cradled the back of her head, angling her until he could deepen the kiss. His tongue possessed her even as he pulled her shirt free from her jeans, slipping up a hand to curl possessively around one breast.

His thumb and forefinger closed over her nipple, pinching lightly through the thin fabric of her bra. She moaned into his mouth, pleasure streaking through her as he bent lower. Kissing his way down her neck, nibbling and licking until goose bumps rose.

Troy broke away long enough to strip away their shirts and her bra. Their breathing echoed loudly in the darkness, and she reached forward with eager hands to stroke his firm body.

"Yes. Fuck *yeah*. Use your nails," he ordered, catching her wrists so he could press her hands harder to his chest. Nic dragged her fingers over his ribs and the firm muscles on the sides of his body as his groan of pleasure rang in her ears.

He moved back until he could cup her breasts, and a moment later his tongue was teasing her. Circling one nipple over and over before switching to the other side.

She dragged her fingers over his shoulders and up his neck until she could bury them in his hair. Then she tightened her fingers to fists, fighting to keep him in one place for long enough.

"Stop teasing," she begged.

For once the bastard listened. Lips closed around the aching peak, he sucked hard. A lightning bolt shot from his mouth to intensify the heat sizzling between her legs.

Suddenly his hand was there, over her jeans as he cupped her intimately. He continued to torment her breasts, but his fingers were opening her pants, sliding down the zipper. Pushing the fabric from her hips so he could jam a hand under the elastic of her panties.

He eased a finger through her curls, lightly floating over

her clit as he separated her and pressed the tip of his finger into her sex.

His ragged breath shuddered over her skin. "You're so damn wet, Nic. So soft, and hot, and I want to sink into you over and over."

"Oh God, *yes*." Nicole slid her legs apart as far as the pants bunched around her knees would let her.

That tempting, annoying, not nearly enough touch between her legs vanished as Troy removed his hand. She would've whimpered in dismay at the loss, except seconds later he was jerking down her panties, pulling off one of her boots and freeing her from her pant leg.

When he put his hand back and pressed his finger into her again, Nic sighed happily. "Do it," she whispered.

His mouth settled over hers, not as frantic as before but just as demanding. Kisses that stole her breath and sent her heart racing as she rocked futilely against his hand.

One finger barely teased her opening. Around and around, with gentle swoops upward to steal a gentle brush over her clit. Not nearly enough pressure. Not nearly often enough.

When he pulled his mouth away from hers, Nic clung to his shoulders for balance, the solid wood door behind her back the only thing keeping her vertical. "Cock tease."

He chuckled lightly. "I think you've got your terms wrong."

"You're a freak," she muttered. "Now fuck me."

"Not yet. But I'll do this."

She gasped as that finger he'd been taunting her with became two, and they were no longer hovering at the edge of her body but pressed as deep as they could go. The shock of it made her clench around his thick fingers, which sent off another quivering tingle.

"So damn hot," Troy murmured, catching her ear lobe with his teeth and biting down lightly. "You like this, baby? Or maybe this?"

Option one, he slipped his fingers nearly out of her body then plunged them back in. Option two, he stayed right where he was, fingers buried in her core but pressed his thumb on her clit as if he were setting off a trigger.

Oh God, she was going to die. *Both.* She wanted both at the same time.

The bastard stopped. Nicole opened her eyes, but it was too dark to see him. She could picture the expression on his face, though, cocky and demanding.

"Tell me, Nic, or I'll stay right here."

Nic let her head fall back against the door with a *clunk.* "I want your cock," she whispered.

If it came down to having to say what she really wanted, she might as well be honest.

It seemed to be the right answer because Troy swore softly. He covered her lips with his and restarted the motion of his thumb. Pleasure, tight but growing, spiraled deep in her core. She held onto him, the heat of his naked torso passing to her palms as she stroked, undulating against him as best she could.

Little noises escaped her throat as she closed in on a climax, but right before she went over, Troy jerked his hand away.

The protest on her lips died as she heard a condom wrapper rip open, and faster than she thought possible, he had lifted her bare leg over his hip, opening her to him.

His cock pressed against her sex, and Troy rocked between her legs a couple of times. She balanced on one leg, reaching down to guide his now-wet erection to where she desperately needed it.

A second later he pushed forward, thick heat stretching her, desire rising fast. He was panting, strong fingers reaching to catch hold of her ass as he lifted her into the perfect position and thrust forward all the way.

"*Troy.*" How she held back from screaming, she wasn't sure. Nicole wrapped her arms around his shoulders and held on tight as he pulled his hips back.

Slow motion at first. Every inch of him sliding deep, every inch pulling away. Over and over, like he'd promised. The room was pitch dark, with the faint sound of music from the party drifting through the thick door. Far louder was the sound of their bodies slapping together as Troy increased his speed.

Their breathing echoed like the beat of a drum. The trembling moan of pleasure on her lips became a melody line. A low sound of satisfaction rumbled deep in Troy's chest.

And over it all, pure, sweet pleasure hovered just out of reach.

Troy adjusted position, leaning her against the door again, but this time when he thrust, his body dragged over her clit perfectly, and Nicole saw stars against the darkness.

"*That.* Do that again," she begged.

For once in his bloody life, Troy listened. He fucked her hard, and deep, and relentlessly until her whole world was reduced to the cock driving into her sex, and the white wall of pleasure breaking over her.

Her sex clenched. Troy gasped, shuddering to a halt. He jerked her leg even higher, pressing deeper. His cock seemed to grow thicker, wrenching another wave of climax from her body as she squeezed his heavy length.

Aftershocks struck in series, each one arching her toward him helplessly. Troy held her steady, whispering soft words as he stroked her heated skin. Careful fingers caressed the side of her face followed by the back of his knuckles trailing down her neck and over her breasts.

Silence rang in her ears.

The scent of cleaners grew heavier as their breathing slowed, and she was left in that satisfied and content post-coital state he was so good at getting her to. Troy carefully lowered her leg to the floor before pressing his lips to hers for a tender kiss, far gentler than they'd shared yet that night.

She held his neck and kissed him back, sighing sadly as he pulled away to deal with the condom.

He chuckled softly. "Damn, I forgot. There's no light switch in here."

"Don't tell me you've been in here before." Nicole turned to the door and ran a hand up and down the wall beside it. "Weird."

"Yeah, it's on the outside. I remember playing hide and seek in the house when I was little. You okay to get dressed in the dark?"

"Well, I'm not about to haul ass into the hallway and get dressed out there," she muttered, the reality of what they'd done sinking in.

Guilt arrived first, followed by disappointment.

As good as the sex had been, she wasn't supposed to be fooling around with Troy. And the idea of going back out and making small talk with Darrell for the rest of the evening—

She yanked her clothes into place. Silently, because there wasn't really anything she could say. It wasn't Troy's fault. It was her own, and now she had to deal with the consequences.

Being responsible was turning out to be a royal pain in the butt.

She was reaching for the door when his strong hands caught her hips.

"Are you mad?" Troy asked, no teasing in his voice.

Nicole hesitated. Blaming him would be nice, but it wouldn't be honest. "No."

Maybe she would've said more, but the door opened behind her, swinging inward. Troy jerked her out of the way, pulling her against him and the back wall as light streamed in from the hall.

A very shocked Laurel stood framed in the doorway, glancing back and forth between the two of them. Her new friend blinked a couple of times before her lips twitched. "I think this is one of those moments when synchronicity exceeds serendipity."

Something suspiciously like a snort escaped Troy. "Can I get you anything? A mop? Dutch cleanser?"

"Full-service closets. They do have everything in this house." Laurel held out a hand, pointing to one side. "Extra paper towels, please. They're on that shelf to your right."

Troy turned to grab the towels, and Nicole took the opportunity to escape, dodging past Laurel and unashamedly hiding behind her.

The instant the paper towels were in her friend's hand, Nicole took off, grabbing her other hand and tugging her down the hallway the opposite direction from the kitchen. They ducked into a bathroom, Nicole double-checking no one, i.e., *Troy*, was following them before turning to face Laurel.

Her new friend stood patiently, her hint of a smile so much less condemning than it should be.

"You okay?" Laurel asked.

Nicole breathed a sigh of relief, even as a dull pain began pounding in her head. "I'm an idiot. That's pretty much the entire explanation."

Laurel shook her head. "You don't need to explain, but if you need a hand, let me know."

Damn it. Nicole kicked her own butt. Not only was she an idiot for letting herself get carried away with Troy, now she was going to be even ruder, because there was no way she was going back to her date.

"Could you let Darrell know I..."

I just fucked someone else, and the party is over? Gee, that would go over well.

Her new friend interrupted her mulling. "I'll tell him you had to go home. The simpler, the better, I think."

"I guess," Nicole agreed.

"Also, I don't like lying," Laurel admitted. "I'm not very good at it."

Nicole impulsively offered a hug, which Laurel returned hesitantly, patting her back gently before slipping out with a soft admonition for Nic to take care of herself.

She glanced into the mirror, horrified to discover what would have been obvious to Laurel and anyone else who saw her. Her lips were swollen from Troy's kisses, her cheeks flushed. She'd gotten all her clothes back on, but it sure looked as if she'd gotten dressed in the dark after a very thorough fucking.

But the worst thing was her eyes shone with satisfaction far more than guilt. Nicole swore as she turned away. At least her body could have the decency of sharing her internal struggle, but it seemed she was too sated to be decent.

It hadn't been boring, her brain pointed out.

Fuck off, she muttered at herself.

CHAPTER 5

After a night like that she should have ended up wracked with guilt, focused on how terrible she'd been to drop all her convictions and get involved, again, with Troy.

Nope. Nicole slept like the dead, totally relaxed in dreamless slumber until her sister Cyndi phoned at nine a.m. and invited her for lunch. That gave her three hours to spend power cleaning her tiny house, burning through the guilt that finally arrived with a vengeance.

Sure, Troy had provoked her, but she'd poked back. If she wanted to change her life, she had to stop taking the bait. No matter how tasty it looked.

Damn the man for being so tasty.

She stopped on the way to her sister's to buy some celebratory flowers at the local shop on Main Street. "With extra carnations and baby's breath, please."

"It'll be about fifteen minutes," the florist warned. "I've got three bouquets to finish up in time for a wedding, but if you want to come back at the top of the hour, I'll have yours ready."

"No problem."

It meant she had time to wander down the sidewalk and window shop. Peek in at the shoe store. Slip into the hardware store and buy a lawn sprinkler/soaker hose thing for her nephews to enjoy over the summer.

She paused outside the Stitching Post Quilting Shop, staring at the display in the window of summer-toned baby quilts with appliqued teddy bears and brightly coloured balloons.

The last time she'd sewn was years ago in Home Ec, and she'd gotten a B minus on her sturdy cotton apron. No way should she be tempted to buy anything that required more handwork than a stapler or duct tape could solve.

She turned toward the street, a strange itch between her shoulders. As if she was being watched...

It had to be her imagination. Nicole shook it off and decided she might as well give in. She slipped into the store, a small chime overhead announcing her arrival.

Warm colours greeted her, along with two smiling faces, one familiar, one not.

"Hi, Nic." Hope Coleman rose from where she was cutting out large circles of fabric, and the dark-haired stranger moved to take her place. "Are you here to pick up Jodie's purse? She forgot it last night after the quilting session."

"I wasn't, but I can take it. I'll drop it off on my way to lunch."

Hope disappeared into a small room off the back, returning with a well-worn and very sturdy purse the size of a grocery shopping bag.

Nic laughed. "How on earth did Jodie forget she had that with her?"

"You'd be amazed what gets left behind at the end of an

evening." Hope offered a smile. "So, if that's not what brought you in, are you looking for something specific?"

"Not sure." Awkward. "What's the simplest baby quilt you've got?"

Hope crooked a finger her way. "Come with me, my pretty. I've got just the thing for you."

"You're scaring me," Nicole warned, both of them laughing.

The bell rang again, and they turned to the door. Troy Thompson strolled in as if him fabric shopping was the most natural thing in the world. His gaze drifted over the store content until it landed on her and Hope, his face brightening as if he'd won the lottery.

"Well, what a surprise."

"To find Hope in her quilt shop?" Nicole deadpanned. "Nice try, Thompson."

"Hush," Hope mock whispered. "What's up, Troy?"

"Looking for a...what did you call it last time? A ragtime quilt kit."

Hope's face lit up. "Another one?"

"Yup."

She looked delighted, as if what he'd said made any sense in English, motioning with her head toward the far side of the store. "This way."

He followed obediently, and Nicole found herself admiring the way he prowled through the tall narrow shelves, long and lean as he closed the distance between them.

Hope had vanished by the time he reached her side, and Nicole stood there, mesmerized, staring into Troy's face. His laughing eyes flashed, a hint of shadow darkening his jawline.

"You didn't shave." What a stupid comment to make. Why had she even noticed?

"Nope." He caught her hand and rubbed her knuckles against his scruff. "Like it?"

She snatched her hand away. "No."

Yes. Oh God, yes.

Her body buzzed, the desire to have him rub his face all over her naked skin far too strong.

"Nic. You come as well. This is what I was going to show you."

Hope's words made her blink, breaking the siren spell he'd cast over her. Troy just smiled his wicked, tempting smile and motioned her forward.

Somehow she ended up leaving the shop with a kit to make a baby quilt. A matching one to what Troy had purchased after talking knowledgeably with Hope about seam allowances and backstitching.

Nicole felt a little dazed. Maybe she hadn't slept as well last night as she'd thought.

"How do you know so much about quilting?" she demanded.

Troy shrugged. "Hope gave us lessons a few years back —the year she set up the charity-quilt thing. Even my dad chipped in."

"And now you quilt just for shits and giggles?"

He laughed. "No. The last time Katy got pregnant I saw her eyeing these things and figured it was a shiny enough gift for the auspicious occasion."

Nicole eyed him, gears turning, not quite believing it. "You made a quilt."

"Uh-huh. It's pretty simple. I can give you a hand with yours, if you want. Sounds as if Cyndi and Katy are expecting about the same time."

Now it made more sense. "You're making another quilt because Katy's pregnant."

One of his brows rose. "You feeling okay?"

No, now that he mentioned it. She was confused, and annoyed, and the proud owner of a bunch of material she was pretty much obligated to struggle with sometime over the next eight months.

Life was peachy.

"You want to grab a bite?" Troy asked, tossing his shopping bag into the back of his truck, which was parked right outside the shop.

Nicole shook her head, walking quickly toward the flower shop. "I'm headed to Cyndi's."

"Pass on my congrats," he said. "What about supper?"

She jerked to a stop, turning to look him over carefully. "What is *wrong* with you?"

"Nothing." His smile widened. "Want me to prove it?"

Jeez, she'd walked into that one. Nicole pinched the bridge of her nose. "Troy, we're not doing this. It's over."

"That's what you said before. I enjoyed it being *over*. I look forward to it being *over* again, since 'over' is your new code word for sex."

"It's not a code word for anything, you *jackass*," she shouted, pulling back in time before she swung her quilt kit at his head. She whirled on her heel and took off, not trusting herself to say anything more without shrieking.

Of course he followed. She couldn't get away from him, even if she tried.

He would have followed her into the flower shop except she deliberately pulled him to the side to try one last time. "Troy. Last night was..."

He opened his mouth, and she pressed a finger over his lips.

"No. No talking."

He tried a slow, burning smolder instead.

Nicole prayed for patience. "No trying to seduce me. And no licking my finger," she said even as his lips opened.

He smiled wryly. "You're no fun today."

See, her brain pounced on his announcement. *Told you. Boring.*

Shut up, shut up, shut up.

She took a deep breath. "I had a blast last night, but it's not going to happen again. I mean it, so you need to move on and get out of my face."

He stood there like a muscular wall, looking down at her with those dark eyes that were far too astute—seeing clear inside her to where confusion continued to roil.

This needed to happen. The weight of the bag in her hands steadied her resolve. If she wanted someone to eventually make a baby quilt for *her*, she needed to leave her wild ways behind.

"Please." She sounded desperate, even to her own ears, but she didn't know what else to say.

His smile faded, and the teasing, tormenting Troy vanished. He looked as serious as she'd ever seen him.

Silence hung on the air between them, then he dipped his chin. "Okay. Okay, you're right. I'll see you 'round."

His fingers ghosted over her cheek, a soft, lingering caress a second before he turned and walked away.

It should have felt like a victory, but she had no energy to cheer. Something inside her seemed to have broken, and sharp edges were poking into her gut, making it tough to breathe.

Brilliant, her brain taunted.

She didn't have the energy to tell herself to shut up.

THE NEXT WEEK DISAPPEARED, and the next, although Troy would have been hard-pressed to give an account of what he'd done during the time.

No. He would have to admit to one thing. He'd found himself far too often doing a one-eighty when he discovered himself seconds away from interrupting Nicole.

He had a damn GPS tracker magically keyed in on her location. It was the most annoying thing in the world to turn the corner at the grocery store and discover her leaning a hip against the freezer compartment, chatting with some guy.

And every time he walked away, it left a foul taste in his mouth.

Didn't matter if he spotted her doing something that made sense, like when he pulled into the gas station and found her getting help checking her tire pressure. It was completely above board for her to be wandering after Damon Jules, the thirty-something dude who owned the station, as he explained how to use the pressure gauge.

Although she should have just come down to the shop and let him or his brothers take care of it...

Troy focused on the rapidly clicking gas meter, ignoring the flirting going on twenty feet away from him. Damon was an okay guy, he guessed. Older. Serious. Ready to settle down, probably.

Only as far as Troy knew, Damon wasn't much in the smarts department. Also, old *old* fashioned, as in he'd once made a comment about women and "their place" in the home. And while Nic might be looking to start a family, Troy couldn't picture her being happy doing nothing but housekeeping and cooking for a husband who planned to come home at the end of every day, put his feet up and spend all evening watching TV.

That was the worst part. Bumping into her all the time meant he saw the guys she was dating, and none of them were right for her. Not that there was a huge selection of possibilities in the small town.

He sat in the café across from Mike, wondering if *any* guy in Rocky was good enough for her.

"You look like you're going to get sick," his friend taunted. "Doesn't say much for the daily special."

"It's from having to stare at your ugly mug," Troy retorted. "That's a pretty sour expression you're wearing."

Mike offered a twisted smile. "Nic's driving me mad."

Good to know he wasn't the only one. "What's she done now?"

His friend hesitated. "I hate the guys she's seeing, but it's reaching the point I can't keep interfering. Last night she threatened to castrate me."

"That's nothing new."

"She was holding a butcher knife when she said it," Mike offered wearily. "Life was so much easier before she got on this dating kick."

Troy agreed one hundred percent.

"I guess it's time for me to let her be in charge." Mike stirred another spoonful of sugar into his coffee. "She'll figure it out. She's smart enough to know who's good for her."

Everything in Troy itched to deny it based solely on the guys he'd seen her with lately.

"Maybe she needs to sign up for one of those online dating places," Mike commented. "Would give her some—"

"Are you out of your freaking mind?" Troy demanded. "Have you seen the kind of bullshit that goes on in those places? You really want her getting pictures of guys' junk from all over the country?"

Mike glared at him. "Not everyone online is an asshole."

"I thought you were trying to protect her, not hook her up with some ax murderer."

"I think they screen out the ax murderers," Mike deadpanned.

The idea made his skin crawl. "Still think it's a bad idea."

"I know." His friend nodded. "You're right."

The conversation lingered in his brain far too long. Even a day later when he was at the shop working with Mitch, he was still trying to come up with the answer.

Where could Nicole find someone good enough for her?

"Are you planning to stand there all day staring at that wrench, or can you get your ass over here and put it to work?"

Troy shook himself alert, glancing over at his brother who was smirking in his direction. "Sorry."

Mitch frowned. "You feeling okay?"

"Fine, why?"

Mitch took the wrench from him then leaned over to loosen the bolts. "You're not nearly as talkative as usual."

"Lot on my mind."

His brother didn't say anything for a second. "Something wrong?"

Everything. Nothing.

Troy ignored the dilemma of Nicole for a moment, and instead gave voice to one of his other concerns. "Is everything okay between you and Anna?"

Mitch twisted the wrench harder than he should have and swore as the bolt snapped in two. The shaft remained jammed in position while the head fell to the concrete floor with a metallic rattle. "Shit. Get me a pair of pliers."

Troy grabbed the tool, bumping his brother out of the way. "Let me get this. I've got a more subtle touch," he taunted.

"You keep telling yourself that," Mitch muttered.

"So, you and Anna?"

Mitch said nothing for a minute.

"Your Len impression is good," Troy said. "Only he doesn't glower as hard as you."

"Shithead."

"Ass." The insults were as natural as breathing and calmed the waters. Troy had been worried since he'd caught them fighting. "You going to tell me what's up?"

Mitch checked around the shop, but the other guys were either outside the open bay doors or in the main office. "She's being stubborn over something important."

"She'd hardly be stubborn over something stupid," Troy pointed out. "She's smarter than that."

"You'd think, but this is different. This time she's wrong."

Troy held his tongue. "About what?"

Mitch sighed as he leaned a hip against the car. "We're thinking about kids, but she refuses to put in for a desk job."

More kids. They were haunting him.

He examined Mitch's face. His brother was dead serious, and dead concerned. "You want her to put in for a desk job now, or after she's pregnant?"

"As soon as she's pregnant. She thinks she should go at least half—" Mitch frowned deeper. "Hang on. You don't seem surprised about the kid thing."

"I'm not." Or not since Nicole had knocked a simple fact into him, hard. "I figured it out the other day. Her family and ours are mostly settled down. The next stage seems to be kids, and with Katy and Gage working on number two—well, I figured it wouldn't be long before everyone's thoughts turned that way. And once there's something in the water, every woman in the area will get the itch."

"Yeah." Mitch offered him a twisted grin. "If there was ever a time for you to practice safe sex, it's now, little bro."

"Tell me about it." Troy managed to remove the broken piece, tossing it aside and going for the next bolt. "Except Janey and Len won't be jumping on the band wagon."

Mitch paused. "Yeah, I guess you're right. Never heard her talk about wanting kids."

"Never heard *you* talk about it either."

"It was never on my radar until Anna," Mitch confessed. "I still don't know how the hell I could possibly be someone's dad, but if Gage can do it and make it look like fun, maybe it won't be so bad."

It was wicked, but being horrible was required in the little-brother handbook. "I can see you now, sitting through parent-teacher interviews. Asking for extra homework for Mitch Junior. Or bailing him out of detention."

"*Fuck.*" His brother's eyes narrowed. "You evil bastard. It's bad enough to think of dealing with babies. I don't need to imagine teenaged versions of me."

Troy patted his brother's shoulder on the way to the workbench. "Don't worry, we survived taking care of you. I'm sure you can figure it out as you go along."

"Ass," Mitch muttered softly.

Troy grinned, then considered. "I don't think you need to worry about Anna. They have a bunch of rules regarding what active RCMP need to be able to do on patrol. Plus, she's not going to put a baby in danger."

"Yeah, I suppose." Mitch gave him a searching look. "I don't know why I told you this in the first place."

"Because you tell me everything, eventually." Troy put on his most endearing smile. "Everyone does."

"Yeah, bullshit on that." His brother tossed him the part they needed, then motioned to get back to work.

It's funny how even with the truth trotted right out in front of them, his brothers didn't seem to notice. Mitch *did* tell him everything. Clay and Len as well. Sometimes it took a bunch of prodding, but over the years Troy had learned to read his family well.

He didn't need to start a conversation with Clay to know him and Maggie were probably also heading down the kid route. He didn't need to ask to know Janey's parents were giving them grief about living together. Or that Janey didn't give a damn about making things official between her and Len, or that Len only cared about making Janey happy. If that meant getting married, Len would have had her in front of the justice of the peace within a week.

Hell, he even knew things like Katy wasn't nearly as sick this go-round, but instead of being happy about it, she was worried that something was wrong with the baby. At least until he'd casually dropped in and let her talk to him about it until she'd decided maybe she was having a girl this time around and the hormone thing was the difference.

Troy knew his family. He knew how to make them happy, and how to ease their fears. That ache inside was still there, though. The one he got every time he thought about Nicole.

Goddammit, he missed her.

Yeah, he knew his family, but it seemed he didn't know how to make *himself* happy.

CHAPTER 6

Things ramped up to high speed for the summer, and Troy was working his ass off. Falling into bed at the end of every day was the only thing keeping him from turning his damn truck around and ending up in Nicole's driveway.

He'd just finished three different backbreaking jobs in the shop before getting called to go haul some trucks out of a mud bog. The teenage drivers hadn't quite figured out that the concept of mud bogging was to *avoid* getting stuck. Or if you did, get your own ass out of trouble.

A group of a half-dozen youth with their jeans muddy to the knees stood sheepishly to one side as he drove up. Four trucks were buried past their hubcaps in stinking, sticky sludge.

Troy was covered with mud by the time he'd gotten the last one out, and was in no mood to answer yet another call from the shop.

"What?" he growled into the radio.

His oldest brother laughed. "I take it you've enjoyed your day?"

"Goddamn princesses were barely old enough to see over the fucking steering wheels. I had to wade into a fucking slough to hook up because the brainiacs forgot to leave one truck free to haul the others out. I need a damn shower."

"Been there, done that. Sucks. I'm sorry, but you're in the neighbourhood to take care of this call, and you might be able to fix it on the spot. Car stalled by Logan's corner. Guy knows nothing about vehicles, so he could be out of gas for all I know."

"Jeez, what the hell is he doing this direction?" There was nothing out here except idiots with oversized trucks looking to tear up government land, or planning to camp for free tucked back into the heavily wooded area a few kilometres to the west.

"Touring the countryside?" The radio buzzed with static for a moment. "Mitch's shouting at me. You got it?"

"Yeah, I can be there in about five minutes."

He was grumpy in the first place, he'd admit that. But when not two minutes later he spotted someone walking on the road toward town, and recognized Nicole, he wasn't as polite as he could have been.

He stopped in the middle of the road and rolled down his window. "What the hell are you doing?"

The frown on her face deepened. "None of your business."

No. Fucking. Way.

Troy was out of the truck and in front of her, blocking her path in under five seconds. "Just out for a stroll, were you, sweetheart?"

Nicole glared at him before letting out a heavy sigh. "Don't get pissy with me. I'm not in the mood for it."

It took all his concentration to keep control of his anger.

"Answer me. Where's your car? How did you get way the hell out here?"

She folded her arms over her chest. "I was on a date, okay?"

"You seem to have lost him," Troy pointed out, sarcasm dripping from every word. "I take it his car broke down?"

A quick nod, but she wouldn't meet his eyes, and now he wasn't pissed, he was borderline furious.

He carefully caught hold of her upper arm, twisting her toward him so he could lift her chin until she had to look him in the eyes. "If you don't tell me why you're out here, I'm going to assume the worst, which means I'm going to kill someone."

"He didn't do anything," Nicole insisted, only her nose wrinkled a moment later as a low admission escaped her. "Well, not *much*."

The fucker was a dead man walking.

"Get in the truck." Troy spoke quietly, pushing her toward the door.

This time Nicole caught hold of him, fingers digging into his biceps. "I mean it. He's a jackass, but that's it. You're *not* allowed to go and rip off his arms."

"He was enough of a jackass to make you willing to walk an hour and a half back to town," Troy snarled.

"I didn't want to wait with him, okay?" She shook his arms, which had about as much effect as if she'd hit him with a bag of feathers. He waited, unmoving, for her to continue. "He was pretty..." her cheeks flashed red "... handsy, that's all."

Troy rolled on past furious to white-hot anger.

"Get in the truck," he said softly.

It must have finally registered how near the edge he'd

been pushed. She moved like lightning, settling in the passenger seat and doing up her seatbelt without a word.

They sat in silence until he spotted a car ahead of them. It was tucked off the road in amongst some trees. A nice private spot to park and fool around, which was fine as long as everyone had the same agenda.

Ice flowed through Troy's veins. "You swear I don't need to kill him."

"No. I swear."

"If I find out later you're lying, I will find him and bury him. Alive." Announced as if he were telling her about the latest fishing trip he'd taken.

"I swear, Troy. He was a jerk for not stopping the first time I asked him to, but I might have overreacted, walking away," Nicole answered quietly. "Please don't do something foolish."

Define foolish. Troy pulled the tow truck to a stop, reaching behind him for a bottle of water.

"Stay in the cab," he ordered before dropping to the ground and pacing the narrow dirt road to where the fellow leaned against the bumper, hood raised, as if he'd known what to check for.

The guy was somewhat familiar, but not anyone Troy had spent a lot of time with. Joshua? Jordan? That.

Nic's date smiled as he came to his feet, apparently not aware he was seconds away from pain. "Good timing. I thought I'd be out here for hours."

Troy walked past him and leaned over the engine. "What happened?"

"Oh, she just died." Jordan paused. "I parked her, and when I went to restart, the engine wouldn't turn over."

"Strange place to park." Even. Calm.

Jordan laughed. "It seemed like a nice quiet spot, only my date wasn't as eager as I hoped."

Troy waited, but nothing more was offered. No comment from Jordan regarding the location of his missing date. No concern about her walking away, nothing.

Final score—zero. Troy ripped out the cables connecting the spark plugs and stepped back, closing the hood with one hand. "You got a cell phone?"

Jordan nodded. "Shitty reception out here, though. It took ages to reach your shop."

Troy pulled a pen from his pocket and wrote a number on the label of the water bottle before tossing it to the other man.

"Thanks, but what's this for?"

"Number for the garage in Drayton Valley." Troy pointed to the ridge about a mile down the road, farther out of town. "You might have better luck getting reception from up there."

Then he turned and walked back toward the tow truck.

"Hey. What the hell are you doing?" Jordan pounded after him, grabbing hold of his arm. "You can't just leave—"

Troy whirled on him, catching hold of the man by the throat. "Be thankful I'm leaving you breathing."

He tossed Jordan aside, the other man scrambling away as he stared wide-eyed at Troy. "You're insane."

Troy climbed up into the tow truck and put it in gear, ignoring the shouting and the rude hand signal Jordan held in the air as Troy spun tires and left the other man in a cloud of dust.

EERIE SILENCE HUNG in the cab.

Nicole wasn't stupid. She wasn't about to say a word until she had to. Which meant during the twenty-minute trip back to the garage, neither of them spoke.

He parked in the back, coming around and meeting her before she could escape. For the first time she noticed his clothes were caked with mud, a dark smear of it along one of his cheekbones.

"Will you be in trouble for not bringing him in?" she asked quietly.

"No law says we have to take a job if we don't want it." He caught her by the arm and tugged her toward the back fence. "We need to talk."

She walked with him through the gate to where they had a little more privacy. A tall fence separated them from the garage work area, and to the west was the open field connected to Katy and Gage's yard.

"Where did you find that winner?"

The words ground out as if he was still clenching his teeth, and she sighed. "He works with my brother-in-law in the environment offices."

"Does Dale know he's an asshole?"

The last thing she wanted to do was defend the jerk, but Troy's coldness broke through and made her snap. "No, it seems to be a recent development."

"Bullshit." Troy stepped into her personal space. "Assholes don't bloom overnight, babe. They're always there, waiting to be exposed."

"You're so gross." But all her bluster had escaped, and she couldn't help herself. She stared up at him, and some of her frustration escaped in a long sigh. "Why do I suck so bad at this? Dating. Finding someone to get serious about."

It took a minute for him to relax, but then he guided her a few steps farther to where the Thompson family had put a bench. He settled, the wood creaking under his weight as he patted the spot next to him. "You don't suck at it. It's hard—I get that."

"Damn near impossible," she muttered. "You know what it's like. You've lived in Rocky all your life. There're always a few new people, but pretty much everyone else, we've known forever."

"There's got to be some good people moving into town," he insisted. "You just need to find them."

She pulled her feet up on the bench and wrapped her arms around her knees, resting her chin on top so she could stare out over the field beside Katy and Gage's house. A sea of tiny blue flowers spread like dashes of reflected sky all around the edges of their yard. "Traders Pub is hosting a speed-dating session this coming Thursday night. I wasn't going to go, but I guess I should."

He didn't comment about that, just gave her the lecture she'd already given herself a dozen times over the last hour. "Set up your future dates in public places. Mike is going to have a bird when he finds out what happened today."

She was on her feet in an instant, both hands landing on his shoulders as she narrowed her gaze. "You will *not* tell Mike."

"No, I won't," he agreed.

What was going on? "Then why would Mike have a bird if he's not going to find out?"

"Oh, I didn't say he wouldn't find out. I said *I* wouldn't tell him. Dale, on the other hand, will probably have a few choice thoughts on the matter."

He wouldn't. "You're *not* going to tell my brother-in-law about my disastrous date."

"Right again," Troy said, wrapping his hands around

her hips and pulling her into his lap. "I won't tell him, *you* will."

Not fucking likely.

"Sweetheart, you need to let your brother know what happened, even if it's just for the sake of the women who work with the jerk."

Shit. She hadn't thought about that.

"He's not a criminal," she insisted.

"No, but, he's an asshole, and he didn't stop right away when you said no." Troy reached up and brushed a finger over her cheekbone. "You're strong, and you're smart, and you've got just enough *don't give a damn* to get out before things got dangerous. Someone else might not be as lucky."

She nodded, letting out a long unhappy breath before leaning toward him and resting her head on his chest. She snuck her arms around his torso. "That is going to be one hell of an awkward conversation."

"If you want backup, let me know," he offered, curling his arms around her and holding her tight.

It felt right to be wrapped up together with him. For the first time since she'd walked out on Jordan, she felt as if she could breathe. It took a few minutes, but some of the tension in Troy's body faded. He'd been so worked up, and it was good to know he was returning to a normal state of mind as well.

"Thank you for coming to get me."

He stroked her hair, the familiar touch soothingly good in all the ways she needed at that moment. "Anytime, babe. Anytime."

CHAPTER 7

Nicole slipped into the passenger seat of Laurel's teeny car. "Sorry I'm late."

"You're on time," Laurel assured her, heading down the road toward Traders. She glanced over. "You look pretty."

"I feel like an idiot," Nicole protested. "I couldn't figure out if I was supposed to dress up or dress down or what. Speed dating. Ugh."

"I doubt it matters the specifics what you're wearing. You get, what? Five minutes at a time? The guys won't notice more than your smile and your boobs, not necessarily in that order."

Nicole laughed. "I can't tell if you say these things on purpose to shock me, or if it's part of your natural charm."

Laurel made a rude noise. "Trust me, the inappropriate comments come naturally. I'm trying really hard to turn over a new leaf and *stop* speaking before I think."

"I'm trying to cut down on swearing," Nicole confessed. Along with the whole lot of other bad habits, but even as they headed toward another step in her dating adventures, Nicole wasn't sure this was the right decision.

Her run-in with Mr. Handsy the other day had been a very unpleasant wake-up call. It wasn't going to be as easy as she'd hoped to change her path. Her sisters had made it look easy, but then, Nicole hadn't been paying much attention when they'd starting dating—she probably hadn't noticed Cyndi and Jodie dealing with bullshit until they found their Mr. Rights.

She was committed to at least try the evening.

A quick peek at Laurel made her pause. "You don't look as if you plan to take part tonight."

Laurel's pale cheeks flushed. "I changed my mind. I'm not looking for anyone to date."

"Oh, *really*." Nicole twisted in her seat, interested in what was causing her friend's blush to continue to rise. "Is that because there's someone you've got your eye on?"

Laurel indicated a turn, her full attention on the road.

"You do. You have the hots for someone already," Nicole teased.

"Have you ever tried speed dating before?" Laurel asked.

"Nice try, but changing the subject isn't going to work. Who is he?"

A low melodic whistle began as Laurel pursed her lips and ignored the question again.

This was getting fun. Nicole leaned an elbow on the dash and grinned. "Come on, you must tell me."

"Get used to disappointment."

"We could double date," Nicole offered enticingly.

Nothing worked. They were pulling into the parking lot at the pub, and Laurel *still* hadn't shared a name.

Nicole was impressed. "You might be a lousy liar, but you're good at keeping secrets."

Laura flashed a smile. "Give me a call when you're done, and I'll come get you."

"You could've told me to drive myself, you know."

"Are you kidding?" Laurel passed Nicole an envelope, leaning across the passenger seat to offer it.

"What's this?" Nicole asked, shaking it lightly.

"A list of questions to ask. I did a Google search for you." Her smile widened. "I figured you might not have thought about preparing."

Nicole checked the first couple of questions. *What do you do for work? Where are you from?*

It looked innocent enough. "Thanks. Great idea."

"You're welcome. And I expect *all* the dirt when you're done."

It was good to know the evening would be entertaining for one of them, no matter what. "Troublemaker."

Nicole passed through the doors on the side of the pub that held the pool tables and dartboards. Usually the room was set up with a mess of tables scattered everywhere for people to sit and chat while they drank. The dance floor and more active entertainments were on the opposite side of the building, separated by a wall.

Tonight the owners had rearranged everything, pulling every small table they had into a wide circle. Two chairs were arranged on either side so that each couple would have a moderate amount of privacy during their short opportunity to talk.

Low music played in the background, and the lights were dim enough all Nicole could see from the corner where the men had congregated were tall outlines and broad shoulders.

"You must be Nicole."

She turned to face the speaker. A pretty young woman dressed in a frilly blouse held a clipboard in front of her. Her blonde hair was held back in a ponytail, and a pair of frameless glasses perched on her nose.

"I am. Nicole Adams."

The woman checked off her name then motioned her to the right side of the room. "I'll be your hostess for the evening. If you'd like a drink, you've got about five minutes before we'll be getting started."

Nicole grabbed a glass of white wine, chatting with a few familiar women. All too soon they were corralled toward the chairs, ladies sitting on the inside of the circle. The position meant that unless she craned her neck all the way to the left or right, she couldn't very easily see the couples on either side of her. Her main focus would be whoever sat opposite her.

She took another sip of her drink, replacing it carefully on the table. Butterflies danced in her stomach, so she grabbed the notes Laurel had made, unfolding the paper in her lap like a talisman, cool and smooth under her fingertips.

"Ladies and gentlemen, we'll be starting the timer in two minutes." Their hostess spoke quietly over a microphone, her pleasant voice breaking through the low murmur of masculine conversation. "Gentlemen, if you could please make your way to your assigned starting position. You'll have five minutes with each date. I'll ask the gentlemen to please move quickly when you hear the bell ring. You'll know it's time to change seats when you hear this sound."

A light, pixie-like noise rang over the speakers, and Nicole fought to keep from giggling. It was too much like the children's book she'd just listened to her nieces reading on their iPad. The one where Tinker Bell rang a bell when it was time to turn the page.

She was still grinning widely when an older man settled into the seat across the table.

The bell rang, and they exchanged names. Nicole glanced at her cheat sheet. "What do you do for work?" she asked.

"Farm."

Nicole waited, but that was the extent of his answer. He seemed extraordinarily pleased with it, though, smiling across at her as his gaze drifted over her face then down the front of her shirt.

Boobs and smile. Nicole was going to hit Laurel hard the next time she saw her for putting the thought into her head.

It took forever before he spoke. "Do you like horses?"

"Not really," Nicole admitted. "I like looking at them, but I don't ride."

His smile vanished. "Oh."

Silence.

So much for the concept of *speed* dating. This was the longest five minutes of her entire life. Turning to see how everyone else was doing would be extremely rude, so she was stuck, desperately, for ways to make time pass quicker.

To the cheat sheet. "Was there something you wanted to tell me about yourself?" Nicole asked frantically.

He thought for a second. "*I* like horses."

Of *course* he did. "Any type in particular?"

His eyes narrowed. "You making fun of me?"

"Oh, no. Honestly *no*." If a hole had opened in the floor at that moment and swallowed her, chair and all, Nicole would've been eternally grateful.

Silence. Then, "Brown ones, I guess."

She bit her lips to stop from laughing out loud. Tinker

Bell *finally* rang the fucking bell, and Nicole breathed a sigh of relief as Farmer John rose, dipped his chin once then shuffled to his right, hat held in hands.

Only fifty-five more minutes of this scintillating, oh-so-entertaining evening to go.

She reached for her wineglass, drinking deeply before leaning forward to replace it on the table and meeting the eyes of her next date—

Troy Thompson sat center stage, eyes set once again to *smolder*.

IT WAS AMAZING how suddenly a mind-blowing revelation could overtake a man.

There he'd been, just a few days ago. Holding Nic in his arms to soothe her even as he fought the temptation to go back and run over Jordan a few times with the tow truck. It seemed so damn stupid that no one in the entire town recognized exactly what a jewel they had in Nicole.

No one but him...

When he'd been about twelve years old, he'd been standing in the garage next to a tall stack of tires. For whatever reason, the entire thing had begun to lean toward him, and he hadn't noticed until the weight was so far off balance, there was no time to escape. It had crashed down on him—inevitable and body-impacting.

Just like the truth did at that moment. There was no one in Rocky good enough for Nicole except...

Well, honestly, no one but *him*.

So here they were, in the middle of Traders, her staring back with just enough anger in her eyes to send a flush to her cheeks, and he was about to become her own personal set of tires.

So to speak.

"What the hell are you doing?" she demanded.

"Innovative question," he said with admiration. "I'm currently taking part in a delightful endeavour called *speed dating*, where the goal is to ask questions to discover if the person sitting across from you is someone you'd like to get to know better for a meaningful relationship."

"So fucking full of beans," she muttered.

Full steam ahead. "What's the most important thing to you in a relationship?" Troy asked.

"We're not doing this," Nicole snapped. "We're not playing some bullshit game just because you want to."

Troy pointed a finger at her. "Hey, I paid my money to be here, same as you. Seems as if you could at least *try* to be polite, and answer my questions."

"*Fine.*" Nicole leaned back in her chair and folded her arms across her chest. "Have it your way. I want a relationship where my partner knows family is number one."

"Good to know." Troy leaned his elbows on the table. "Personally, though, I'd put my partner first and family second. Because it's got to be the two of us and what *we* need first. Family comes after that."

She stopped and seemed to consider what he had said. "Huh."

"Surprised?"

"Yes. I didn't know jackasses could talk." Nicole ignored his chuckle, instead glancing into her lap. She brought a piece of paper to the edge of the table, reading rapidly. "What's one thing about you that you'd like me to know?"

"I'm exactly the man you're looking for."

A choked gurgle escaped her. "Can you be serious for even two seconds?"

"Baby, I'm serious as hell. Ask another question."

She glanced down. "How long did your last committed relationship last?" Her head jerked up, and a tight, condemning smile appeared. "Answer *that* one, Thompson."

He reached across the table and caught her fingers in his. "Since January, I've been involved with an amazing woman. I haven't seen anyone other than her since then, so that makes it over six months and counting."

Her jaw dropped slightly, lips hanging open. "We're *not* in a relationship, Troy." She jerked her fingers free from his grasp. "Why are you doing this?"

"Because out of all the people you've been considering in your plot to move on to the next great thing, you forgot to consider me." Troy shrugged slightly. "It was a natural mistake, since I'm so shy and retiring, I just thought I'd help you come to your senses."

"Come to my—?"

The buzzer went off to signal the end of the session, and Nicole leaned back as if she'd gotten a reprieve from a death sentence.

Only Troy wasn't going anywhere.

He glared at the man who stood waiting beside his chair. "I'm not done yet," Troy said. "Take the next seat."

"But that's not how—"

"I said take the next seat," Troy snarled before turning back to Nicole and giving her his full attention. Speaking with utter politeness. "Next question on your list."

She glanced around to see if anyone was watching them. The guy Troy had commandeered his spot from had listened, moving on to chat with the woman beside them.

"I don't know what you're trying to prove here, Troy, but it's not funny."

"Do I look like I'm laughing?" Troy lowered his voice. "Sweetheart, I'm serious. I think you and me could be damn good together, and I want you to give us a shot."

She stared at him, something in her eyes giving him hope for a split second before she stiffened, pulling out her notes. "Do you want to get married?" she read off the sheet.

He really should have resisted. "I thought you'd never ask."

"*Troy.*"

He grinned. "Yes, I want to get married. I used to think getting married wasn't necessary, but then I realized it was the actual wedding part that sucks."

She lost her sarcasm for a moment. "Really? Marriage is okay, but it's the *wedding* that's bad?"

"Pretty much. It's stupid to spend that much time and energy going crazy for one day, when you'd be better off saving your money and putting the effort into something that's supposed to last a lifetime."

Hazel-green eyes stared unblinkingly.

"Ask me the next question, Nic."

She swallowed. "What do you like to do for fun?"

"Sex is good."

She glanced around before glaring again.

He kept going. "But not just any kind of sex. My favourite kind is the spur of the moment, where I lose my head because I'm so into you and giving you pleasure. Like, it's not enough for me to hold you while we watch TV. I want to stroke your skin and play with your hair. I'd touch you over and over, and when you sigh and start to relax into me, I'd roll you to the couch and start kissing you everywhere. Kissing, licking, and nibbling until you're screaming with pleasure—"

"Troy, stop it this instant," she hissed.

He pressed his hands to the table and leaned in closer. "I'd be watching, just like I'm watching now. Because your body would tell me what you want more of. The pulse in your throat beating so hard I can see it, your breathing picking up. I'd run my finger down your naked body and ask you if you wanted me, and you'd say yes."

The buzzer rang.

This time all it took was a glare to make the next guy keep walking so Troy could get back to convincing Nicole he was all she needed.

The momentary pause had been enough to let her rally her control. She sat straighter, her expression full of confidence. "I see what you're doing, but this isn't going to work, Troy."

"No?"

She shook her head. "Because all I need to do is ask you *one* specific question off this sheet, and you'll run for the hills with your tail between your legs."

"Hit me with your best shot."

"Where do you see yourself in five years?"

"Small house somewhere here in Rocky. Hopefully on the edge of town so it's quiet, but still close enough to get to the garage where I work with my family." Her expression didn't change, but he hadn't gotten to the good part yet. "We'd be together for nearly six years by that point. We'd have at least two kids, and probably a dog, and—"

Nicole rose to her feet, grabbed her purse and left.

Troy raced after her, ignoring the questioning glances from the other couples at the tables. He waved away the organizer, rushing out the door to discover Nicole standing at the edge of the stairs, her arms wrapped around her body as she stared into the parking lot in frustration.

He stepped in front of her.

"Go away," she ordered, voice brittle as if she were holding back tears. She looked to the side, avoiding his eyes.

She was trembling. He pressed his hands to her upper arms to steady her. "I'm not going anywhere."

"Of course you're not. You're just going to get in my face and keep hounding me even though you know it's not what I want."

"You really want to do this here? Right out in the open where anybody could run into us?"

"No." The word snapped at him like a wet towel.

Neither did he. He needed time and a quiet place so he could convince her he'd made the most important decision of his entire life. "I'll meet you at your house."

She sighed. "I need a ride. I didn't drive."

The distance to his truck stretched out seemingly for miles. She ignored his helping hand and crawled into the cab, stared out the window and ignored him.

Troy drove in silence. Heck, he didn't say a word the entire time it took to drive, park, then cross the distance to her back door. Nicole fumbled in the fading light for her key.

He waited until they were safely in her living room to start his full-on attack. "I didn't show up tonight to be a pain in your ass—"

"Too bad," she muttered, "because you did a *fabulous* job."

"Do you mind?"

"Oh, was I interrupting?" She gestured grandly for him to proceed. "By all means, please continue."

He let her sarcasm slip this time. "I finally woke up and clued in after we talked the other day."

"What huge revelation overtook your life, and apparently mine?"

He guided her to the couch before sitting on the edge of the coffee table in front of her. "You said you needed to move on. That it was time to take the next step, and I realized I want to be the man who takes those steps with you."

"Troy, you're not making any sense."

"Why? Because I'm not allowed to change? That doesn't seem fair. If you can decide it's time to grow up and move on, then I can as well."

"Yes, I suppose. But it doesn't mean we're going to move on *together*," she insisted.

"Again, why not?"

"Because you're not the kind of guy a girl gets involved with when she wants to settle down and start a family." Her volume increased as the words raced out.

"I *wasn't* that kind of guy. Just like you weren't that type of girl. If we're going to change, we may as well change together."

She raised her hands and pressed her fingers against her temples. "You're not listening. Or maybe I'm not smart enough to explain it."

He circled her wrists and brought her hands into his lap. He stroked her fingers with his, soothing best he could. "Deep breath and try again. What type of guy does this new girl get involved with, then, if not someone like me?"

Nicole stared at where he touched her, his thumb caressing the back of her knuckles. "If I go by my sisters, someone who is dead serious about the people in their lives. Settled, with a solid job."

"If you dare say 'quiet and laidback' I'm going to laugh in your face, you know," Troy warned.

She waved a hand. "I know my family lives at *mosh pit at a rock concert* volume, but they're solid when it comes to being there for each other. They don't do things on a whim. They plan."

For fuck's sake. "Spontaneity is not evil, Nic. Just because we enjoy life, you and me, it doesn't mean we can't be in a full-time, committed relationship."

"That's not the way I see it."

"Then give me a chance to *make* you see it," he said. "What would it hurt for you and me to officially date and try to make a go of it?"

"It wouldn't work," Nicole insisted. "I need someone who is committed to family, and nothing about your life has been about family. Well, you've got a great family, and I know you care about them, but you haven't had to be *there* for them."

"That's not true. Not by a long shot," he growled, annoyance and anger pushed down so he didn't lose his focus.

"You can't argue with history, Troy." She squeezed his fingers then slipped her hands free from his. "Maybe you're right about the spontaneity versus planning thing, but you not being reliable is a deal breaker."

"Bullshit."

"No shit," she snapped back. "And that's not to mention the biggest deal breaker of them all. It's all good and fine for you to offer me some sweet fairy tale about a white picket fence with two point five kids and a dog running around in the backyard. You straight-up tell me, Troy Thompson. You ready to have babies?"

"Physically, I think you're the one who has to have them."

She shot to her feet, towering over him as she planted both fists on her hips. "Stop joking around and answer the damn question. And don't tell me what I want to hear, tell me the honest truth."

Anger simmered, low and steady. She didn't think he'd done shit for his family, because he'd always kept his actions quiet. He hadn't wanted anyone to know he was stepping in, trying to make a difference, and now him being a sly bastard was coming back to bite him on the ass.

"Honest truth?" He ignored the other aching hurt and focused on this one issue. "I'm still a little shaky on the baby thing, but I know the first part is one hundred percent solid. I want to be with *you*, Nic. I want us to be together, and I want us to do the next thing at the right time. I don't think *any* guy would say, 'Hell, yeah, let's go make a baby' the instant you got involved."

"So you can't say you honestly want kids," she declared triumphantly.

"No. I mean, *yes*. I mean, dammit, I *think* I want kids, but I'm glad it would take at least nine months for one to arrive, because am I ready to be a dad this instant? Hell, no. But I don't think, if you're being *honest*, you'd be all flipped-out happy if you could hit a button and have a kid pop into your arms, *bazinga*."

She was still standing over him with fire in her eyes, only her lips were twitching.

"What?" he complained.

Nicole sniffed lightly, fighting her amusement. "*Bazinga?* Really?"

"Not the right sound effect?"

She shook her head as a smile finally broke free. "God, you are a special kind of frustrating, Troy Thompson."

"Likewise, Ms. Adams."

"We're probably going to kill each other, you know."

His heart gave a jolt. "Lame special-effects aside, does that mean we're going out? Officially?"

One final moment of hesitation before she nodded. "Fine. We'll give it a shot. It's not as if I've got a long line of Prince Charmings waiting to sweep me off my feet."

"Not unless you want to learn how to ride brown horses," Troy offered, excitement rushing through him and making his head light.

Her mouth hung open. "Troy Thompson, you were *eavesdropping*."

"Of course I was. I wasn't about to let my girlfriend be swept off her feet by some eager-beaver farmer who might seduce her by taking her to see his fertilizer pile."

Her lashes fluttered. "Girlfriend?"

"*Girlfriend*." Troy rose and decisively gathered her into his arms. He lowered his voice, seductive and urgent at the same time. "I think we need to make it official, don't you?"

He stroked her cheek, drifting his hand back until his fingers were buried in her hair. He'd do everything in his power to make them work, and he was willing to play dirty. He cupped the back of her head, tilting her neck as he stared hungrily at her lips.

Her breathing stuttered to a halt as she stared back.

Good thing dirty was going to be so much fun.

He smiled as he lowered his head.

She'd walked into a trap.

Unwittingly at first, but the longer Troy pushed, the more giving in to his nonsense made sense.

And now, with him looking at her as if he'd discovered a new flavour of ice cream, there was no alternative. She'd go along with his suggestion until the whole situation fell apart and even *he* had to admit that they were the wrong combination to try for forever.

At that point she'd probably have to up and leave town to find what she needed, because it was obvious Rocky was a dead-end for her, partner-wise.

But for now? His hand was hot against her skin. Nearly as hot as the pounding pressure inside her core as he stared hungrily. They were going to have sex. Which wouldn't be boring, because sex with Troy was the opposite of boring.

Thank God, her brain squeezed out before her synapses could be scrambled by rapidly developing lust.

"I'm going to kiss you," he warned needlessly. He held her motionless, bringing up his free hand to stroke his fingers over her cheek. Outlining the shape of her lips. "Over and over again."

"*Yes.*"

His lips curled into a wicked smile. "You're going to like this," he promised.

Yes. Yes, she would.

He waited, touching and teasing, like he'd done during the speed dating. His talk about sex had set her squirming in her seat, and she'd have given anything at that moment to get him to back off.

Only now he didn't need to hesitate. There was no reason for him to be moving so slowly.

"Anytime," Nicole encouraged. "If you haven't forgotten how."

"It's not a case of forgetting," Troy murmured. "I've never done this before, and I want to make sure I get it exactly right."

She rapidly dismissed the obviously wrong answers to his "never done this before". He'd kissed a woman before. *They'd* kissed before... Hell, they'd *done* it all before.

"Nope," she confessed, an involuntary shiver sweeping her as his fingers trailed down her neck to tease along the edge of her V-neck shirt. Fingertips hot against her skin. "You got me on that one, Troy. *What* haven't you done before?"

He tightened his grip and leaned forward ever so slightly. "I've never kissed a serious girlfriend."

His lips brushed hers. Gently. And again. Far too softly to be the cause of her heart rate soaring as much as it did. She sounded breathless when she spoke. "Don't worry. I'm fairly confident you can make it up as you go along."

His tongue traced the seam of her lips for one brief moment before he pulled away again. "I don't know.

Expectations are high. Plus, I've got too many options. Should it be slow and sweet until I make you tremble? Or should I kiss you like we're on fire, and the only thing that can put out the flames is to burn up all the oxygen in the room?"

Nicole leaned forward, attempting to press them together, but he resisted. He held her steady, with the hand at her neck countered by the rock-solid grip on her hip. He eased his body back half an inch, which was enough to set them brushing together, but not in full contact. Heat wrapped around them, far more seductive and nerve tingling than an outright, blatant grind.

"You're driving me crazy," Nicole muttered.

"Payback. And ditto."

He'd snuck his thumb under the bottom edge of her T-shirt, and as he kissed her again, he stroked the skin at her waist. The rest of his fingers were linked through the belt loop of her jeans, and it was apparent he wasn't going anywhere, but that small motion combined with the touch of his lips—

She was drowning in sensation. Craving more. Going wild from sensory overload triggered by two small connections.

"Kisses." Troy spoke against her lips, breath mingling with hers so she breathed him in. As if he couldn't bear to pull away any farther. "So many kinds," he said.

Nicole pressed forward harder. Urging him to increase his assault.

He fisted his fingers at the back of her head, tangling them in her hair and using it to control her. The small tug of pain made her gasp even as her nipples tightened and a hard pulse set off between her legs.

"Uh-uh," he warned. "That's not an option tonight."

Jeez, he really was trying to kill her. "You're punishing me for dating other guys," she guessed.

He shook his head, stroking the skin at her waist like a touchstone. "I'm rewarding you for saying yes to dating me."

"I'm on board for sex," Nicole pointed out. "We're pretty good at it, and it's a lot of fun."

"It is. It's one of my favourite things, in fact. But we're waiting."

The buzzing need inside her flared in protest. If they could have, her brain and body would have cried out melodramatically in unison like a heroine in an old-fashioned novel.

Nooooooooooo.

"Tell me you're kidding," she pleaded.

He kissed her. Harder this time. More like the demanding and body-sating Troy she was familiar with. She clutched at him, striving to untuck his T-shirt from his jeans, but he caught her wrists and held her still. Lips moving over hers, his tongue took possession as he utterly and completely devastated her senses.

Once again, he pulled back. "Not kidding."

Nicole dropped her forehead against his chest, breathing heavily. "You know, I'm pretty much a sure thing tonight."

He chuckled. "Only we both want more than one night, baby."

Damn him. He had her so mixed up she didn't know which way she was going. "No sex—is that what you're saying?"

"We're dating, and I don't fuck on the first date."

Good lord. "Since when?"

"Since now."

Because it meant making her blood boil then leaving her aching. "I know you," Nicole said. "This isn't you."

He hummed as he released her wrists. "Really? Sweetheart, there're a whole lot of things you don't know about me."

Troy was being a bloody brick wall, and she didn't have the energy to fight him anymore. She curled her fingers into the fabric of his shirt, clinging tightly as she looked up and met his dark-brown eyes. "Then I guess it's a good thing we're going to date."

"A very good thing."

She smoothed her palms down his shirt before taking a step back. They stood a foot apart now, the living room light shining on his face, clearly illuminating the mischief in his expression.

"You're enjoying this," she accused.

"Immensely." His smile flashed even brighter, and she had to smile in return.

Nicole glanced around the room, the heated frustration inside lingering, but there was something else there as well. Curiosity at the forefront—was it crazy that she loved not knowing what he would do next?

When she glanced back, Troy was gazing at her with something unreadable in his expression. Hope? Fear? Something far more serious than she remembered seeing there before.

The odds of this thing between them working was maybe forty-sixty, and not in their favour. The only item she could completely agree with him about was how hot the sexual attraction between them burned.

Maybe skipping the sex would make it clear quicker that they were flogging a dead horse with the relationship attempt.

"Okay. No sex tonight."

"Damn. I was looking forward to doing unspeakable things to get you to agree with me."

A laugh bubbled up, slipping past the tension and making her shoulders relax. "And here I agreed because you were refusing to do unspeakable things to me."

"Good point." Troy cupped her face in his hands. "Don't worry," he reassured her. "We'll get back to the dirty, unspeakable things soon enough."

"Promises, promises."

"Yes, a promise."

He kissed her again, and this time Nicole didn't try to speed them up. Instead, she used all her senses to soak in every sensation possible.

The five o'clock shadow on his jaw scratched against her skin as he fluttered kisses to her ear. His breathing grew unsteady as he traced his tongue over her skin, heated air brushing past her. Cheek to cheek, he took hold of her earlobe and sucked it into his mouth, biting down lightly.

His hands rested on her hips, while hers were pressed to his torso. Like a living rock wall against her palms, his chest rose and fell as he explored his way back to her lips. Her entire body tingled, but she wasn't sure if it was from a lack of oxygen or the potent taste of him racing through her system.

As a first-date kiss, this one ranked *way* the hell up there.

When he pulled back, she swayed toward him, just for a second before she pressed herself back to vertical, staring into his face.

His eyes seemed unfocused, as if he was as shocked by the impact as she was.

"I should be going," he said softly.

Nicole nodded, not trusting herself to respond. Not until he made it to the door, ready to leave. Then he turned, a more familiar teasing smile in place, even as determination shone in his eyes.

"What time do you want me to pick you up tomorrow night?" he asked.

A shiver of dread struck. They were really going to do this. They were really going to make it official and go out somewhere in public.

Oh. God.

"Yeah, I know," he said.

"Did I say that out loud?" she asked in a panic.

He shook his head. "Your face. It pretty much matched what I was thinking."

"We're asking for nothing but trouble," Nicole warned.

"Good thing we like trouble," Troy returned. "Traders. We'll go dancing."

She swallowed hard and pulled in her courage. If they were going to do this, they might as well do it right. "Come for supper first. I have leftover lasagna in the freezer."

His smile widened. "I'm going to like this dating deal."

"It's not *that* good of a lasagna," Nicole deadpanned.

Instead of laughing, he stood there, his hand on the door, hesitating for far too long, his expression growing more serious until he swore.

"Ah, *fuck it*—"

He closed the distance between them, snapping her into his arms and laying siege to her lips. This time with as much passion as they'd ever shared. She couldn't breathe, she couldn't see. All she could do was accept the rising pleasure as he controlled her senses and made her ignite from the inside out.

Suddenly his grip on her loosened, and he turned on his

heel and left. The door swung shut before she'd had time to take her first gasping breath.

Nicole staggered forward, hand against the doorframe as Troy hurried to his truck, escaping as if he knew speed was vital. As if he had to leave now or he would change his mind about everything, and they'd end up naked in the next five seconds.

She raised her hand to the glass in the door, heart pounding, a smile on her lips.

It was good to know they were tormenting each other.

Troy drove straight home, still in pain by the time he pulled into his parking stall. He sat there taking deep breaths to try to clear his head.

His brain ached. His cock ached. His *body* ached from how hard he'd been clenching his muscles to stay in control as he'd kissed Nicole. Kisses only, and nothing else.

Yeah, he was a fucking hero.

It was his own fault he was suffering, yet Troy couldn't help but accept the pain as a badge of honour.

They were going to do this—and they were going to do it right.

Except now he was in a quandary. Somehow he needed to convince Nicole they were the perfect couple. In spite of his own worries regarding the future.

The kid thing?

An icy chill raced up his spine. *Yeah*, that idea was still enough to make his blood freeze, but it wasn't as shocking as it would've been a few weeks ago. He'd always considered he'd have his own family off in some foggy, nebulous future.

It seemed the future had begun to arrive.

Frankly, all the other things worried him more. The secrets he'd kept that she needed to know to see him as the right partner for the future.

Only he had no idea how to go about spilling the beans without hurting his family. It wasn't as if he could just up and list what he'd done. Not without sounding egotistical, or seeming to condemn the people he loved.

Maybe he hadn't thought this out as much as he should have.

Troy jogged up the stairs of the second-floor apartment he shared with Mike, dropping his keys on the table inside the door as he headed into the living room.

His step faltered as he discovered his best friend leaning against the back of the couch. Mike's arms were crossed and he was staring at where the ceiling and the wall met, breathing heavily, as if he'd been running.

The whole keeping-secrets thing ran far too deep when it came to his friend. "Hey."

Mike tipped his chin briefly, lips pressed into a narrow line.

Troy stopped. "Did you end up—?"

His best friend exploded off the couch, lunging forward with his arm swinging forward—hard. His fist connected with Troy's face, spinning him around.

Troy raised his hands as he scrambled for a safe position. "What the—"

"You *shit*. I can't believe you have the guts to come marching back in here after what you've done." Mike swung again, fury in his voice.

He was too angry to do more than flail, and Troy ducked under his swing, catching hold of his friend from behind with a death grip over both his arms. "Goddammit, Mike. What the hell is wrong with you?"

An elbow jerked free, and Mike rammed it into his ribs. Troy gasped in pain as Mike whirled and tackled him to the floor. He got in another couple of solid punches before Troy used his heavier weight to get the upper hand, holding Mike down without fighting back, because he knew what this had to be about. Defending himself was one thing—but he wasn't about to beat up his best friend.

He ended up kneeling on his friend's arms to keep from getting his eyes poked out.

"I got word you were being an asshole to Nicole. Something about getting in her face during a social event at Traders," Mike said, fury in his voice. "I said *no way*. I said *Troy would never think of bugging my sister*. So I go over to Nic's, just to see if she needed a little TLC, or something, because obviously the story got twisted by the local gossips."

He heaved his body upward, trying to break free from Troy's grasp.

"I wasn't being an asshole," Troy insisted. "And if you stop trying to plant your fist in my face, I'll let you up so we can talk about this rationally."

"There is no rational. I *saw* you at Nic's place. You were kissing her, you bastard, so now I'm going to rip your throat out."

So much for sitting and talking this through. Troy adjusted his position, leaning more weight on his friend until Mike's attempts to buck him off grew more futile. "There will be no throat ripping, and you know the only reason you landed a single punch is because you got the jump on me."

"Maybe it won't happen tonight, but you're dead," Mike snarled. "Somehow, sometime, when you don't expect it—"

"Oh, stop being a fucking drama queen. What are you? Twelve? Yes, I was kissing your sister. We're dating."

Mike's eyes widened, and his face grew even redder. "No. Fucking. Way."

Sudden exhaustion rolled over Troy. After the rest of his evening, this was the last thing he needed.

Troy rose to his feet, extending a hand to his friend. "I really don't want to have this conversation with my junk being bashed every time you move. Get up, and stop being a jackass."

Mike glared, but he slapped his hand into Troy's, pulling hard to get to his feet. "There's nothing you can say that will make this okay to me. I know what you do with women."

Troy had reached the point of physical exhaustion and mental weariness where everything was bound to set him off. Still, he knew it was a bad idea to let out a snicker. "Really. The same thing you do?"

"Fuck *off*. Not the same thing."

"I haven't heard any complaints from the women I've been with, and hey, you've done a few of them with me at the same time, so what's your problem?"

"Jeez, Troy. Don't you *dare* talk about sex and my sister in the same breath."

"You think she doesn't know about the birds and the bees yet? You *are* a dreamer."

"*Stop talking*," Mike ordered, fists clenched again. "The discussion is not going there. Ignoring the fact you've been with dozens of women, you *can't* date my sister. You're not good enough for her."

Troy understood Mike was pissed, and that he was trying to score hits, but the comment still burned. "I'm good enough to be your friend even though I'm a rotten piece of shit, but I'm not good enough for her?"

"Yes."

Jeez. "If I'm not allowed to date your sister, then who the hell *is* good enough?"

"I don't know, but it's not you." Mike shook out his arms, wiggling his fingers as if his knuckles hurt from smashing into Troy's face. "She said she wanted to get serious, and you're about as serious as a...as a... Hell, I don't even know what to compare you to, because you've never *been* serious."

"Fine. You think I'm dirt. Great. Then you have no choice but to go back to the basics. Like you told me in the café the other day."

Sheer suspicion smeared his friend's expression into a tangle. "What the hell does that mean?"

Troy shrugged. "You said she'd figure it out. That Nic was smart enough to know who's good for her."

"Not if she wants to get involved with you," Mike shouted.

They were talking in circles. Enough already.

"Not your decision." Troy deliberately looked his friend in the eyes. "I'm not doing this to be a jackass. I really like Nic, and I think this can work. But you've got to stay out of our hair, and you've got to give us a chance."

"All sorts of bullshit," Mike muttered. "You're talking out your ass."

"You really think I would do this without having thought about it, *hard*?" Troy demanded. "I figured I was going to get all sorts of grief from you, although the punch to the jaw surprised me."

"I was aiming for your nose," Mike admitted. "Figured if I broke it, you wouldn't be so pretty anymore."

They both collapsed into chairs by the table, groaning as they settled. Various parts of his body tingled with lingering pain.

What a fucking *fantastic* evening this had been so far.

"You sure you want to do this?" His friend shook his head at Troy's instant *yes*. "You know if you hurt her, I *will* kill you, and that's not me being dramatic."

"If I hurt her, I'll take myself out," Troy promised. "But we're going to give it a try, and I honestly think I can make her happy."

Mike shook his fingers again. "Great. Then I guess this means you'll be there tomorrow night at the family dinner."

Troy's stomach fell all the way to the floor before bouncing back up into place. "Tomorrow?"

"Yeah." His friend's eyes gleamed with unholy glee. "Didn't Nic tell you? Birthday party for Dale. *Everyone* will be there. Birthdays are big family events, you know. It's a great place for Nic to introduce her new *boyfriend*."

Facing all of the gossipmongers at Traders seemed a whole lot safer. "I'll talk to Nic. Sounds great," Troy lied.

Mike shoved himself to his feet. "Don't do anything stupid. You treat her right, you got that?"

"Of course."

Troy found himself thinking back to when his little sister Katy had dropped a bomb and announced she was pregnant, then Gage had insisted he was the daddy. That night he would have done more than just punch his future brother-in-law in the face if he'd been given a chance.

Mike was being fairly reasonable, all things considered.

Troy put his hand up to his jaw and rubbed. With any luck, he would avoid having a black eye or too-obvious bruises for tomorrow's *family* dinner.

"By the way," he mentioned casually. "You're pulling your swing when you punch. That's why you hit my jaw."

"Shut up."

"Seriously, the force behind your leverage is good, but you messed up your trajectory."

"Go *away*, before I take a practice swing or two."

Mike stomped toward his bedroom, but he'd cooled off enough Troy figured it was safe to go to sleep without hiding the butcher knives.

Then again...

He took a quick detour through the kitchen before heading to bed.

Seemed dating Nicole was going to be exciting for *so* many reasons.

CHAPTER 9

Troy: *morning, babe*

Nic: *Hey*

Troy: *what time should I pick you up for the party?*

Nic: *???*

Troy: *you know, your BILs birthday*

Nic: *shit*

Troy: *lol, right?*

Nic: *wait. that's Sat*

Troy: *Mike says 2nite.*

Nic: *Oh shit*

Troy: *time?*

Nic: *want to skip it?*

Troy: *are you kidding? I looooooove birthday parties*

Nic: *this is a bad idea—OMG*

Troy: *we'll deal*

Nic: *MIKE told you*

Nic: *what happened?*

Nic: *do I need to kill him?*

Nic: *fuck. I'm so sorry*

Troy: *lol chill. We're cool*
Nic: *was there blood involved?*
Troy: *not much*
Nic: *OMG*
Troy: *only a few stitches*
Nic: *WHAT?*
Troy: *the scar should be barely noticeable*
Nic: *are you being an ass?*
Troy:—

His phone was snatched out of his hands, and he scrambled to grab it back. "*Hey*, I'm in the middle of something."

Clay held the phone to one side, blocking Troy with his other arm as he checked the screen. "I noticed, but what you're *supposed* to be in the middle of is getting a tune-up done on the Chev. Not flirting with...*Nic?*" His brother turned back, surprise in his eyes. "Since when?

Troy shoved Clay's arm out of the way, lunging wildly to return his phone to his possession. "Just happened."

"Wow. Nope, didn't see that one coming." Clay stepped back and folded his arms over his chest. "Whatever. Stop wasting time when you're supposed to be working."

Jeez. "Me taking a few minutes to figure out my plans for tonight isn't any different than you answering your phone and chatting with Maggie."

"Totally different," Clay said.

"Bullshit." Troy raised a brow at his brother. "Why's she been calling so often, anyway? Is she bored because she's got no school stuff to do?"

"She's not calling that often."

Changing tactics was the best way to get Clay's mind off Troy's business. He'd been doing it for years—distracting his big brother, usually for Clay's own good. It made his big brother happy to have someone to take care of, and most of the time, it didn't hurt.

But it was still as necessary as breathing to get in some digs while he could. Troy considered everything he'd learned in the last while and made a calculated guess. "Now that I think of it, the *last* time she called, you hightailed it out of here like your pants were on fire. I wonder what was so urgent that you needed to go at that very minute..."

Clay's eyes narrowed, his lips pressed into a thin line.

"And if I remember correctly, you were smiling pretty damn hard when you came back after lunch."

His brother shuffled uncomfortably.

Oh, this was too good to resist. "Must've been a pretty tasty lunch—"

"Shut up now before I break your face."

Troy tucked his phone away and turned back to the open hood of the truck he was working on. "Don't mind me," he said cheekily. "I won't tell anyone."

"*Troy.*" A world of warning in the single word.

"What?" Troy grinned at his brother. "How come your face is so red, bro? You wouldn't be skipping out on work to get busy, would you?"

"Stop it. I don't know how you figured it out, but yes, we're...trying to get pregnant. And chances are higher if she pays attention to her temperature and all kinds of crazy shit I had no idea about. I figured we'd fool around more, so it's not like I *mind* getting called to come home in the middle of the day..." Clay stuttered to a stop, swearing lightly. "I have no idea why I told you that, and I will rip your head from your shoulders if you dare mention a word of this to anyone, especially Maggie."

Troy laid a hand over his chest and let his jaw drop slightly as if he were shocked by the accusation. "Me? Tease my sweet sister-in-law-to-be? Never. You, on the other hand..."

Clay let out a mighty sigh. "I guess it was too much to hope that no one would notice."

"Around here? I'm surprised the rest of them haven't already clued in." Troy escorted his big brother back to the car Clay had been working on earlier. "All teasing aside, I'm thrilled you guys are going to start a family right away. Tanner needs cousins."

"It's a big step, but we're pretty excited."

"Of course you are. You guys are going to be fantastic parents." Troy patted Clay on the shoulder. "Now, we should both get back to work. No more fooling around, I promise. And if you need me to pull a little extra time, let me know."

"Appreciate that, but it should be fine." Clay was beet red in the face. "Just might need to run out..."

Somehow Troy kept a straight face, giving his brother a two-fingered salute before turning and heading back to the truck. He glanced down casually at the phone he'd swiped from Clay's back pocket. It took less than fifteen seconds to change his brother's password, and another forty-five to upload a new ringtone for Maggie's number.

Troy left the phone on one of the tool chests. Clay would probably figure he'd forgotten it there, at least until the next time Maggie called.

He whistled as he made a big production of grabbing the tools he needed, slipping his own phone out of his pocket to check if Nic had left any more messages to their interrupted conversation.

Nic: *you are being an ass*

Nic: *Troy?*

Nic: *I'm headed into a meeting. Deadzone*

Nic: *if you really want, see you @ 5*

Did he really want to face the entire Adams family at the same time? Of course he did. Tonight was going to be a total blast.

And maybe if he kept telling himself that, it would end up being true.

NICOLE HAD STEWED ALL DAY, but it seemed there was no choice but to brazen this out. Family night at the Adams'. She and Troy would sink or swim from the start.

He showed just before five, jogging up to her back door. He looked a little worse for wear, but none of his limbs were in a cast, and all of them seemed to be accounted for.

"What does Mike look like?" she asked.

"He's fine," Troy assured her. "Let me get that."

She stepped back and let him pick up the enormous box waiting on the counter.

He frowned at the weight and shook it lightly.

"You won't be able to tell what's in it." She motioned him out the door, closing it behind her. "You know this. Family tradition—all gifts are wrapped in completely deceptive ways to keep the giftee guessing."

"Is it safe to put it in the back of the truck?"

Nicole crawled into the passenger seat, holding out her arms. "I'll keep it in my lap."

He ignored her hands, propping the gift on the edge of the truck bed so he could step closer, leaning into the cab and offering a flirtatious smile. "I didn't get my hello kiss."

She'd been so distracted, worrying about where they were headed. "You're right. We definitely need to do something about that."

She twisted on the spot, and he stepped between her knees, pulling her to the seat's edge to put their bodies in full contact. He leaned down and pressed their lips together in a brief, intense connection.

"Hmmm, nice."

He flashed a heated glance her way. "There's more where that came from."

"We should stay here," she suggested, stroking her hand down the front of his body. "It'll be a whole lot more fun."

"No can do. We've got a party to enjoy," he reminded her. He gave her the package then sauntered around the truck and climbed behind the wheel.

Her sister and brother-in-law's was a ten-minute drive on the opposite side of Rocky Mountain House. The rest of the family had already arrived, judging from the cars in the driveway, including Mike, who had just pulled in to park directly in front of them.

They met on the front walkway.

Mike shook his head as he looked them over, Troy carrying the gaudily wrapped present in his arms. "I expected so much more from you, Nic."

"Don't even try it," she ordered. "I'm not in the mood for your bullshit."

"If you're really stuck on playing with him, why not keep him as a pet for a while?" Mike suggested. "He's pretty much housebroken."

"Better than you," Troy taunted. "I'm a gentleman. I know how to put the toilet seat down."

"Fuck off," Mike said, far more mildly than Nicole expected. "One question before we go inside, though."

They stopped, facing him.

He narrowed his eyes. "What the hell did you do with all of the knives?"

Troy's smile extended into a full-out, evil grin. "I'll tell you where they are if you tell me *when* you went looking for them."

Mike hesitated. "Fine. I was going to add a few... creative touches to your leather jacket this morning, but since I couldn't find anything sharper than a toothpick..."

What the hell? "My God, Mike. Don't you dare touch Troy's shit," Nicole sputtered. "Or *Troy* for that matter. This has nothing to do with you."

"Hey." Her brother raised his hands. "I didn't do a thing," he said innocently.

"Only because I hid all the knives in the first place," Troy muttered. "My leather? Seriously, dude? That's dirty. You know how much I love that jacket."

The two of them glared at each other.

Good grief. Nicole clapped her hands rapidly to get their attention. "Well, then, this has been *soooo* much fun. Mike, you *will* behave. Or I'll tell Mom and Dad who set the fire in the dumpster behind the mill when we were twelve."

Her brother blanched. "You wouldn't dare."

"Try. Me." She smiled sweetly before turning and offering her hand to Troy. "Come on, big guy, the party's about to begin."

"Put in your earplugs." He took her hand and let her lead him to the door as Mike hurried ahead of them, a lot quieter than usual.

Blackmail. She didn't pull it out very often, but with a family like hers, it was a necessary insurance policy at times.

"The twins are here," her dad announced from the doorway to the living room.

Whether it was from his years working in the open spaces and noise of the mill, or just his personality, her father had only one volume: big and bold, his deep voice ringing off the walls as if he were calling a rodeo event.

"Hey, Nic. Mike..." He spotted Troy, his smile still firmly in position. "And an extra guest. Troy. How're you doing, son?"

"Great." Troy juggled the gift in his arms as he tried to free his hand to accept the other man's handshake. Nicole rushed to his rescue, pulling the present from him. "Good to see you again, Mr. Adams."

"Brian. You're *more* than old enough to call me Brian," her dad reminded him, volume set to high. "You staying for supper?"

"I was planning—"

"Kevin," her dad roared over his shoulder. "Set another place at the table."

"We already set the table for fourteen," Nic's mom shouted back.

"We need *fifteen*, Mother. Mike brought the Thompson boy with him." Her dad vanished around the corner, continuing to shout instructions.

Oh, hell. Nic glanced at Troy. At her brother.

Mike looked far too pleased as he shrugged. "Hey, I'm not helping. You want him, *you* claim him."

As if Troy was a lost little puppy.

"Fine." She shoved as much annoying sister attitude as she could muster into the single word before turning to her new boyfriend. "Come on, Troy. Time to face the music."

"The entire percussion section," Mike intoned dramatically, "with an extra side of kettle drums."

Nicole took a deep breath then followed her father around the corner into the din.

No one even glanced their way.

Her sisters were bouncing off and on the two couches,

depending if they needed to chase down a kid or not. Her mother sat in her usual easy chair while five kids under the age of four crawled, toddled and otherwise stormed the room, constantly in motion. Nicole's brothers-in-law were rearranging the table, arguing good-naturedly about which side to place the bread plate.

"Mike," Kevin ordered loudly. "Grab another chair from the den."

"Nicole. Good to see you." Dale marched up and wrapped her in a bear hug.

"Happy birthday to my favourite brother-in-law... named Dale," she announced with a flourish.

"Ha. For a minute I thought I'd managed to rise to the top." Dale leaned in close, looking her intently in the eyes. "How are you doing, little sis? Life treating you better lately?"

Oh lord, the conversation she'd had with him about Jordan had been agonizing. He'd been so apologetic, she'd felt horrid.

"I'm okay," she insisted.

"Good. I'm glad to hear it. Now." Dale scooped up son number one, who'd been tugging at his leg to get his attention.

"Daddy?"

"Tyson, will you wait one minute while I finish talking to Auntie Nic?"

Tyson leaned his head on Dale's shoulder, and now Nicole found herself with two sets of identical grey-blue eyes peering intently at her, as if the chaos and noise in the background didn't exist. Only her and whatever Dale wanted to tell her.

Conversations with her brothers-in-law were intense at the best of times.

"Jordan put in for a transfer within Environmental Resources," he said seriously. "Decided he'd prefer to work the north division. You won't see him around town after the summer."

Shit. A little overboard, although there was a sense of relief too. "Was that because of me?"

Dale shook his head. "But I mentioned my concerns to HR, and it turned out there'd been previous complaints of inappropriate behaviour on his record. His new posting keeps him out of the office."

"Then I'm glad he's gone. Thanks for letting me know."

"Anything for my favourite sister-in-law...named Nic." He turned that intense focus on his son. "Now, tiger, what can Daddy do for you?"

Nicole patted his shoulder in farewell as Tyson asked a question about sitting next to someone at the table.

Nicole turned to track down where Troy had gone to while she'd been distracted.

Damn.

He'd been pinned to a wall by her dad as Brian recited in detail the—oft-repeated—play-by-play of the championship game where the local Rocky high-school football team had unexpectedly won the provincial championship.

That had been over eight years ago, and Nicole could recite the conversation because it never changed.

"...and it flew. Picture perfect, that pass. *Ahh*, I can see it now, spiraling through the sky, like a rocket shooting into outer space."

Troy's smile was fixed in place. "Lucky throw," he insisted, like Nicole had heard him say more times than she could count.

"And my Mike—right there, in the clear. That ball just floated into his arms like the angels themselves scooped it up and dropped it along with manna from heaven. *Touchdown.*" Brian threw his arms in the air and roared.

Nicole jerked out of her father's way, narrowly avoiding his swinging arms. She offered Troy a sympathetic smile. He blinked hard then returned his attention to Brian.

If *she* knew all the words to this conversation, Troy had to be sick of hearing them.

"Dad, how about letting Troy grab a drink—?"

"Got him one already," Kevin announced, stopping beside Troy and holding out longnecks.

Damn it. It seemed impossible that the entire world was so oblivious to the fact Troy didn't drink. Ever. But he'd told her before not to make a fuss about it, so once again her dad grabbed one beer and passed the other to Troy who folded his arms, the bottle hanging loosely from his fingers as he leaned harder into the wall. His expression was familiar as well—easygoing. Happy. As if everything in his world was perfect.

He caught her eye and gave just the slightest incline of his head, stilling the words she'd been about to say regarding her family offering him alcohol.

She bit her lip and wondered how he put up with it. Why.

Kevin rolled the conversation forward, shaking his head in disbelief. "Still can't believe you turned down a football scholarship to the U of C."

Troy cleared his throat. "Not everyone knows what they want to do at seventeen."

Her brother-in-law looked... Well, he wasn't rude enough to look disgusted, but it was clear he didn't understand *or* approve of Troy not heading immediately after high school to university.

Nicole had never understood it either. She hadn't left

town until a few years after she'd graduated when working and living twenty four/seven with the family business had become too much to bear. Plus, she'd waited and saved up enough to do what she wanted without their help.

Her family was old-fashioned about some things. Her sisters had worked at the family feed mill until they got married and had kids. As the lone male, Mike would someday take over the business, so he hadn't needed to head to university either. It was stupid and sexist and...what they all knew was going to happen.

Her going away had sent the family into a tailspin the entire time she'd been gone.

But Troy? Fourth son in a family of five meant there seemed to be no logical reason for him not to have jumped on the opportunity.

She would have jumped. Hard and fast. Like he said—he obviously hadn't been ready to do something serious with his life.

"Brian. Stop harassing that boy and let him breathe." Darlene Adams stepped in, one of her granddaughters in her arms. "Also, you need to go carve the roast. Kevin, someone needs changing."

"Isn't that what grandmas are for?" Kevin suggested.

"Nice try, bucko."

She passed little Dara to her dad, and bodies swirled around one another as if they were dancing, headed in different directions as voices ebbed and flowed in the background.

The front doorbell rang, and Troy took advantage of the moment to put his beer on a side table and reach for her, tugging them backward down the hallway.

"Well, this has been fun so far." He stopped beside the

broom closet, his smirk picking up as he tilted his head toward it. "Want to check it out?"

"No." She attempted to stifle her giggles. "Oh God, don't do that to me right now."

"I'm not doing anything. I'd *like* to be," he murmured. "Just a few minutes, sweetheart..."

"Hey, Nicole," Kevin called after them. "Come here. There's someone I want you to meet."

She turned with a smile, figuring he was teasing and had one of her nephews lying in wait. Instead, she looked up at a solid six-foot-four of handsome stranger with deep-blue eyes.

He stood beside her brother-in-law, smiling easily as he extended a hand in greeting. "Chase Pine. You must be Nicole."

"That's me. Nice to meet you." Nicole gestured Troy forward. "Troy Thompson."

"Mike's roommate," Kevin explained as he stepped between her and Troy, draping an arm around her shoulders and guiding her and Chase toward the living room. "So, Nic. Chase is the new man on my crew at the fire hall. Just started this week, but he came from Camrose. Did his training at that college you went to."

"Lakeland?" She faced Chase, pulling to a stop in the open space in front of the door. "I don't remember seeing you."

"Graduated three years ago," he offered.

"Ah, that's why. I started the fall after you left."

"Great school, though. Did you enjoy it?"

"It was perfect. Small enough I didn't get lost, big enough to not be Rocky..."

He laughed. "Small towns. Each one unique, yet somehow exactly the same."

Nicole glanced past him as they talked about their time at college. Kevin had left them, probably to deal with his daughter. Troy…

Troy had settled on the couch next to Mike, but his eyes were fixed intently on her. He wore an expression that was halfway between a smirk and exasperation. She knew *exactly* why it was there.

She nodded at something Chase said, then held up a hand. "Excuse me a minute."

"No problem. I'll save your spot," he teased. Flirtatious, even, and Nicole turned her back and sighed.

She made her way across the house to where Kevin had vanished with Dara, slipping into the room as he was finishing his task.

"Hey. What's with bringing Chase to a family event?" she asked.

Kevin glanced up, bringing Dara to her feet on the bed.

"Great guy, don't you think? I figured he'd enjoy a home-cooked meal and some friendly company. Just being welcoming."

Of course he was. Ninety-nine percent truth, plus the one percent that he'd failed to mention.

"You just happened to invite Chase to a family dinner. And he just *happens* to be single. And went to the same college as me."

"Funny how coincidences happen." Kevin lifted Dara up and kissed her softly. "All ready for dinner, sweetie."

"I don't need to be set up," Nicole warned. "I'm very capable of finding a guy on my own."

"Of course you are," Kevin said as if shocked. "Only if *I* find him for you, then I'll have already vetted him. Makes life simpler."

"You do *not* get to vet my boyfriends," Nicole said sharply as she followed him back into the family area.

Kevin pivoted, pressing a finger over his lips to warn her to keep quiet—*ha!*—just as the dinner bell rang.

A growl of frustration threatened to escape, but she knew her family. They meant well, but they'd run roughshod over her for *her own good* if given the chance. Always had, always would. She loved them for it and simultaneously wanted to shake the lot of them.

"Everyone. To the table," Darlene commanded with a clap of her hands. "Mike, you're over there. Troy, you take that one beside him. Cyndi, you and the..."

Nicole slipped ahead of her brother and dropped into his chair.

"Oh, Nicole. You're over here, please."

Her mom indicated the space next to Chase. Nicole should have taken bets on the seating arrangement.

"No, I'm over here. I don't get to sit beside my buddy Tyson that often," she said with a smile just for her nephew who was already tucked into his booster seat.

It was a reasonable request, not to mention her mom couldn't rearrange the entire table without making it obvious she was trying to seat Chase next to Nicole.

"You're playing with fire," Troy murmured in her ear before leaning past her to offer four-year-old Tyson a fist bump.

No. The point was she didn't *want* to play with fire, not after agreeing to go out with Troy. Didn't matter how nice Chase was according to Kevin. But this was Troy's opportunity to show his stuff, and if he was going to give up at the first sign of a little honest competition...

"You backing out on your 'I want to date you' spiel, Thompson?" she whispered.

Troy glanced across the table at Chase. His jaw tightened, and he twisted back to her, all the fire she'd ever need in his eyes. "Like *hell* I am."

A shiver zipped along her skin, and a small bubble of warmth burst inside. She told herself it was because she was glad he was showing some backbone.

It also might have been that his hand landed on her thigh under the table at that exact second.

"Hey, Chase."

Nicole ripped her gaze from Troy's and snapped her attention to her brother, who'd ended up seated next to their new guest.

"You should see if Nic has time to show you around Traders tomorrow night," Mike offered with an evil glint across the table at Troy.

"Traders?" Chase turned his smile on her again. "Local entertainment?"

"Great place," Troy butted in before Nicole could answer. "Drinks and pub food, games, dancing—you'll like it." He stretched his arm along the back of her chair, playing with her hair as he aimed his best devil-may-care grin across the table. "Nic and I will be there by nine. If you want, we could introduce you around."

CHAPTER 10

Troy had been the center of attention before, many times.

The response he got from the collected Adams family to his not-so-casual comment was way more intense. That penetrating concentration they were known for was impressively scary when aimed all in one direction.

Especially in utter silence.

That bit was unexpected. He didn't think they were capable of anything less than a dull roar.

Still, fourteen faces with widened eyes and slack jaws were a tough act to follow with anything. Until—

"Lovely idea, Troy. So kind of you to offer. Now..." Nic's mom stood decisively and clapped her hands again. "Who's ready for dinner? We have all Dale's favourites, since it's his special day."

He'd expected that. Darlene Adams was the soul of discretion and smoothed the waters because they weren't alone. Only the *look* she gave Nic made it clear there would be further conversation, and soon.

Chase? He clued in fast enough, cracking a ready smile as he glanced between Troy and Nic.

"Can't tomorrow night, but I'll take you up on that sometime." And then damn if he didn't do his best to help ease the situation, turning his focus down the table to invite others to rejoin the conversation. "Speaking of food—how about a list of the top places in town to grab a bite, for the poor stranger who hates to cook."

"Just keep getting invites out to dinner," Mike suggested.

"Great idea. That takes care of once a month."

The family banter went back to moderately normal—loud and cheerful—but the entire time there was this edge. Eyes kept darting toward him and Nic, confusion uppermost in her family's expressions.

Not as if they thought he was an ax murderer or anything, just...concern and disbelief.

"Remind me to kick you in the ass when we get out of here," Nic murmured as she leaned past him to grab a basket of bread.

"I look forward to it," he returned, joining in one conversation after the other for brief moments as everyone resumed their habit of speaking at nearly the same time on a million different topics.

Somehow they got to the end of the meal without anyone straight-up coming out and asking Nic what the heck she was doing, and then there was just the gift opening and birthday cake to get through before he could steal her away.

Dale shook his present from Nic. "You got me a bunch of bricks," he guessed.

She smiled innocently, batting her lashes at him. "Nope."

"A rock collection."

"I take it the box is heavy?" Brian chuckled. "I know! She baked you a cake."

"*Dad,*" Nic complained as the family laughed.

Dale ripped his present open to pull out a bluish-coloured block about a foot square with an envelope tied to the top. "Oh, Nic, you shouldn't have. Just what I've always wanted."

"You have no idea what it is, do you?" Nicole snickered.

He was opening the envelope. "Gift certificate to Timberline Inn. Now *that* I can appreciate." He waved the envelope at Chase. "Best steaks in town."

"I'll remember that." Chase pointed at the brick. "FYI, that is a salt block. If you've got a place to put it, you could get your own steaks down the road."

Dale looked confused. "What do I need with a salt block?" he asked Nic.

"You need it so your gift certificate weighs more than it should," Nic deadpanned.

He shook a finger at her in admiration as he reached for his next present. The plain white envelope Troy had dropped on the side table stood out amongst the rest of the gaudily wrapped and oddly shaped gifts.

Dale turned to him. "From you?"

Troy nodded, leaning back to watch.

Dale ripped open the envelope and pulled out a rectangular note, his face fixed into a polite smile. "It's a certificate from the garage for an oil chang— Wait, it's not." He glanced up at Troy. "It's a gift certificate for *lessons* on how to do an oil change?"

"Ha. Now you won't be able to get out of doing it your-self anymore," Nic approved with a laugh, nudging Troy in the side.

"When it works for you," Troy told him. "If you bring in your truck and Jodie's SUV at different times, I'll go over how to do both of them."

Nic's brother-in-law nodded, his expression changing to slightly more impressed. "Thanks. It's a great gift. I'll give you a call."

Troy waited until the gift unwrapping was done and the cake had been served, but once they'd reached the point where people were taking second helpings, he slipped from his chair and followed Nic who had taken a load of empty dishes to the kitchen.

He caught her by the hand and pulled her with him toward the door. "Come on. It's time to go."

To his surprise, she didn't offer any complaints. They slipped their shoes on and escaped out the back door, sneaking around the side of the house and into his truck before anyone was the wiser.

"I liked your present," Nic said, twisting to face him. "Of course, your offer might come back to haunt you. Dale's ineptitude when it comes to any kind of vehicle mainte-nance is legendary."

"I'll survive." He was pretty proud of himself, actually, to have come up with something spur of the moment that not only was a great gift, but met the Adams family surprise requirement. He glanced at Nic. "You want to wait until we stop driving to give me hell?"

"For announcing we're going out like that?" She shook her head. "I thought about it, and no. You basically took the first opportunity we were given."

"That's what I figured."

"You enjoyed it, though, admit it." Nicole hesitated. "I wasn't trying to keep it secret, you know. I just didn't get a chance to get a word in edgewise with Kevin all gung ho about…" She trailed off as if reluctant to remind him there were other more-approved candidates.

Time to set her at ease. "About trying to set you up with Chase? God, that was hysterical."

"He meant well." Nic tilted her head innocently. "And Chase seems like a nice guy."

"Good-looking too," Troy drawled.

"Oh?" She turned and looked out the front window, deliberately teasing him. "If you say so. I hadn't noticed."

He chuckled but didn't go down that path. As far as the evening had gone, Troy was counting it as a win. "Are you going to get in hell for sneaking away?"

"Nah." She shrugged. "They probably won't notice that we're gone for a while, what with the kids being all wired up from the cake and ice cream. And Jodie is a fanatic about how the dishwasher gets loaded, so I don't even try to help beyond bringing the stuff to the kitchen."

Troy thought about it for a moment before telling her the truth. "I like your family."

An astonished stare greeted him.

"No, seriously. I like them."

"Did you make this decision before or after you decided to drop the bomb?" Nic demanded.

"I've always liked them," Troy insisted. "They live life out loud, literally, and they sometimes jump to conclusions, but they honestly enjoy each other's company, and that's important to me."

Her eyes met his as he pulled the truck to a stop. She was considering his words, and it was clear she couldn't find anything to be judgmental about. "You always have enjoyed your family."

"Of course I have. And yours is pretty awesome, most of the time. Although we'll probably go deaf at a young age."

"Shut up," she said with a laugh as she looked around. "Troy? Why did you bring me to the mill?"

He got out of the truck and came around to open her door, helping her down and then keeping hold of her fingers. "Because originally we said we'd go dancing tonight, but I don't think I can take any more loud activities."

"So, we're at the mill because...?" Nic followed along at his side, her fingers wrapped in his.

"I still want to dance. And this place has the best floor space I know outside of Traders." He led her around to the side door, where he punched in the access code, swinging it open for her to enter first.

"It's all sorts of wrong that you know the access codes," she muttered.

"Your father told me," Troy pointed out. He thought a little harder. "Actually, I think your mother told me as well. And Mike, and...Cyndi? One of your sisters. As an emergency backup, or asking me to pick up things they'd forgotten."

He'd brought her across the wide-open room with the hardwood floor to where an old boom box sat on the counter, a more modern docking station beside it. Troy plugged his phone into the power, hit the playlist he'd prepped that afternoon, and as slow music swirled around them, he caught her in his arms and pulled her against him.

The evening had worked out well, at least relatively. But that sense of frustration remained that he knew he'd have to deal with at some point.

Why was someone like Chase an acceptable prospect for Nic, when he wasn't?

It was hard to stay annoyed, though, with Nic moving against him, her fingers threaded into the hair at the back of his head. A gentle hum escaped her lips as she accompanied the music.

They were more than comfortable together, passion rising as her breasts rubbed his chest. Troy stepped one leg between hers as he pressed a hand against her lower back, keeping their bodies in full contact.

She offered her approval. "It's not our first date anymore."

"Technically, it is," he teased.

Nic dropped her forehead against his chest then sighed dramatically. "Mean and nasty, that's what you are, Troy Thompson."

"Never," he swore. He tapped his fingers under her chin and tilted her head back until he could get at her lips. Brushing their mouths together softly before kissing her.

The country music playing in the background was accompanied by the soft shuffle of their feet over the wooden boards as they kept dancing while they kissed. Languid and lazy at first, Troy tasted her, soaking the flavour and feel of her into his very system.

As always, that faint flutter of attraction he constantly felt around her roared up to full-out desire between one breath and the next. His body hardened, and he pulled back to look into her eyes.

Deep-green pools of desire reflected back at him.

"I'm sorry for the grilling you're going to get from your family about us," he said seriously.

"You're not really going to talk about that right now, are you?" Nic asked, shock in her voice. "Don't you think we have something better we could be doing?"

Troy grinned, crowding her backward toward one of the tall tables at the side of the room. "I just wanted to make it clear what I'm apologizing for."

"Apologizing?"

He reached between them and undid her jeans, both the button and the zipper, peeling the fabric off her hips as she clung to his shoulders for balance. He caught her around the knees then stood, carrying her to the tabletop so he could finish the job of stripping her naked from the waist down.

Then he leaned over her, one hand on either side of the table as he looked down her body, licking his lips as his hunger rose. "You know, I have given this a lot of thought. Us, officially going out."

He leaned over so he could kiss the top of one thigh, smiling as she shivered under him.

"What kind of thought?" Nicole asked breathlessly.

Troy settled back on his heels as he looked up, hands slipping to the top of her knees. "Since this is supposed to be a new start, I considered trying to be less bossy regarding sex, but the more I thought about it, the less appealing that seemed."

He tightened his grip then applied pressure until her legs opened, his head perfectly level with her sex.

"*Oh God.*"

He ignored the little comment, even as it sent his blood racing. She was turned on by the idea.

"Beautiful. You're so beautiful down here," he murmured, leaning forward to press a trail of kisses along her inner thigh. Her legs jerked in his grasp as he closed in on where he wanted to be. Words spoken against her skin. "You'll just have to put up with me being bossy."

As a follow-up to a family dinner, being ravished at the mill made for a dandy dessert. All thoughts of facing the music regarding their relationship were swept aside as Troy took control of the situation.

Which it sounded as if he planned on doing on a regular basis, and every sexual nerve in her body screamed *yes* at high-volume.

Troy knew exactly what she needed, and where she needed, and as she lay on the solid surface of the oversized table, the muscular man moved from kissing her a million places to kissing her one specific place, settling between her legs as his lips and tongue made far too gentle contact with her sex.

A teasing touch. And another. Circling her clitoris before stroking between her folds. Over and over as if she were some kind of exotic ice cream and he was enjoying her on a hot summer day.

Finally his tongue fluttered rapidly, hard enough to build the tension before he eased away.

She moaned with frustration. "I swear, Troy, if you tease me, I will scalp you."

As far as she was concerned, moments like this called for fast and furious, but when he got in a mood, what he'd give her instead was slow and torturous, every move on his part calculated to make her pleasure ebb and rise over and over until she damn near exploded.

Now it was her own fault he eased off pleasuring her, lifting his head so that his dark-brown eyes threw heat her direction as he answered her. "You like what I'm doing?"

"I'd like it more if you'd make me *come*."

"Not ready to do that. But I can do this..." The words slid into a mumble as he lowered his head again, and a million electric shocks raced through her body.

For all his faults, Troy Thompson definitely had the moves.

Nicole gave up fighting. He'd said he was going to be bossy, and every indication showed it was true. And she was fine with it, especially when she knew the reward would be a soul-satisfying orgasm.

She pulled her legs farther apart, and he slipped his hands under her butt, raising her hips as his tongue returned to teasing flicks against her clit. Pleasure rose steadily like the thermometer on a summer day until she broke through the top of the glass, slow undulating waves relaxing her limbs and making her sigh with contentment. She collapsed onto the table and let the aftershocks take her as he slowed his touch, dragging every bit of pleasure from her body he could.

Troy pressed a kiss to the inside of her leg, his deep voice a murmur in her ears. "You taste so fucking good. I can't get enough of you."

He climbed onto the table and covered her with his body, powerful thighs touching hers, his sculpted torso a heated brand against her bare belly where her shirt had been dragged up. He nuzzled her neck, a sexy grumble rolling past her ear. Nicole dragged her fingers over his ribs, stroking the strong muscles, rocking against the firm shaft rubbing against her through his jeans.

"This would be far more pleasant if you were naked," Nicole suggested.

"Stop rushing." He twisted them to an upright position with her straddling his lap. Her bare legs rested on the tabletop, naked sex pressed to the thick length beneath the front of his jeans.

Intimately together, and yet not. And Troy didn't seem to be in any rush to open his pants.

She slid her hands down his sides, headed for the front of his jeans. "Release the kraken," she pronounced dramatically.

Troy chuckled, catching hold of her wrists and pulling her hands behind her back.

"Let the wild beast lie sleeping for a while." He held her steady as he kissed her again, deep and needy. Possessive kisses that stole her breath and made her tingle all over.

Nicole gave up on her agenda and let him call the shots. She ignored the faint burden of guilt caused by receiving a very excellent orgasm from a still-to-climax partner. Troy was a big boy—he knew she was willing and ready for anything.

He'd take what he wanted when he needed it, and what he seemed to want was for her to be absolutely boneless against him. Clinging to his shoulders as his mouth tore all rational thought from her brain.

When he finally let them come up for air, she had a death grip on him. Her fingers were clenched into firm muscles as she met his gaze. Both of their chests heaving. Both of them staring as if the other might spontaneously burst into flames.

"Wow."

It was the most articulate she could be at that moment. In fact, she was pretty impressed she got that much out.

His lips curled upward. "Yeah. Me too."

She didn't understand it when he placed her on her feet, gently pulling her jeans into position, hands dancing over her as he helped straighten her clothing.

The music was still playing, and he pulled her back into his arms for another dance. He was hard against her, but he smiled and sang along with the words, twirling her from one song to the next, as if he was perfectly delighted with the results of the evening.

It wasn't what she'd expected, but it was pretty damn amazing.

Nicole looked up at the man she'd known most of her life and wondered if she really knew Troy Thompson as well as she'd thought.

Nicole stepped out of the bathroom after her morning shower and jerked to a stop. The scent of banana-and-chocolate muffins wafted on the air, causing her mouth to water and her heart to momentarily skip a beat.

She was the only one home, and she hadn't put anything in the oven.

Grabbing clothes from the chair beside her bed, she stuck her head into the hall, listening hard as she jerked a sweatshirt over her head. The coffeemaker was running, and there were feminine voices in her living room—low whispers that were all too familiar.

Good lord, she'd been invaded. Nicole couldn't wait to hear them explain this one.

A minute later she was dressed, rounding the corner into the living room to catch Cyndi and Jodie in full-out war-strategy planning mode. Or at least that's what it looked like as they snapped short sentences at each other, barely audible, their lack of usual volume made up for by excessive hand and arm swinging.

"Morning," she offered. "Hope I'm not interrupting anything."

"Morning, sweetie." Cyndi jumped to her feet and held out her hands. "You look lovely this morning."

Nic held back her amusement. "My very favourite pair of holey yoga pants and matching sweatshirt. I'm ready for my portfolio shoot."

Her sisters glanced at each other, then back at Nicole, like twin owls caught in a bright light.

Beep beep.

Jodie shot into motion, rushing past her to the kitchen. "And the muffins are ready. You want coffee? Of course you do."

"Of course. What else could I want on a Saturday morning than to drink coffee and hang out with my sisters?"

"And eat banana muffins," Cyndi reminded her. "Your favourite."

"Let's not forget the muffins." Nicole was merciless. She knew what was coming. Didn't mean she'd make it any easier on them.

Jodie lowered a tray to the coffee table then handed Nicole a cup of coffee. "Single, single."

"Speaking of *single...*" Cyndi said brightly.

Nicole and Jodie groaned.

Cyndi wrinkled her nose. "Too cheesy?"

"*Way* too cheesy," Jodie informed her, settling on the couch and primly nibbling a muffin. "Let the girl drink."

Nicole made herself comfy in her favourite armchair, legs tucked up, muffin balanced on the wide armrest. She took a deep drink, letting the caffeine soak into her system as Cyndi and Jodie discussed everything from swimming lessons for their kids to what was growing in their gardens to the latest gossip. It was a moment of calm in the midst of the storm, and it was exactly where Nicole wanted to be, even though she knew the coming discussion was going to be annoying to the nth degree.

"You finally awake?" Cyndi teased as Nicole relaxed back into her chair.

Nicole smiled into her coffee cup. "Of course."

Instant reaction. Jodie leaned forward, placing her plate on the table. "We want to talk to you."

Snickering inside. "Of course."

Every time she repeated the words, she changed her tone of voice. This time she went for "bright and expectant", to differentiate it from the previous times when she'd used "casual indifference" and "long-suffering patience".

And with that, the J and C show took off at high speed.

"We noticed last night—"

"It seemed as if—"

"Well, he as much as *said* it—"

"We just wondered if you'd considered—"

"Because we *were* surprised—"

"Totally surprised—"

"Not that he's a *bad* person."

"Not at all—"

"But we were *surprised*—"

"*Totally* surprised."

They fell silent. Staring at Nicole.

Blink.

Blink.

Nicole held herself as motionless as possible, but she still felt her lips twitch. "Was there a question in all that? Or a statement? Maybe you should try again, only one at a time, please."

"It seems you've been having trouble lately with...men," Cyndi said boldly.

"Not that Jordan was your fault," Jodie rushed to assure her. "Still, maybe you should try dating Chase before he gets snapped up."

"Yes, oh hell, yes." Cyndi's eyes widened and she shook a finger at Nicole. "He *is* new in town. Date him first before you give up."

"I *haven't* given up," Nicole insisted. "And he seemed very nice, but I'm happy to be seeing Troy right now."

Jodie's nose wrinkled. "Yes, we saw that and he's nice..."

"Very nice," Cyndi agreed. "He's not... Not..."

"Not very grounded," Jodie offered.

Not so many hours ago Nicole had said almost the same thing to Troy, but hearing her sisters say it made her uncomfortable. "He's got a steady job," she pointed out. "Has had for years."

"Yes..." Cyndi made a face. "At the family garage."

Nicole raised a brow. "Don't tell me his job is undignified, or some such bullshit. Our family makes a living serving farmers and ranchers. And both of you worked there until you had kids."

"Oh, it's not that at all." Jodie looked horrified. "He seems to float through life, Nicole. Nothing hits him."

"Is he working there because he loves it, or because it's simpler than *finding* a job he loves?" Cyndi demanded.

"We want you to be happy," Jodie said again. "And that means long term. In our opinion, Troy Thompson isn't the kind of man who'll be there for you, long term."

It was nothing she hadn't said herself, yet it didn't sit right to hear it from others.

"Maybe he's changed. Changing," Nicole offered.

"You sure you want to test drive the beta version?" Cyndi leaned forward and placed a hand on her knee. "Hon, he's not a forever man."

Her other sister was nodding in agreement. "Troy is...a sweet boy."

Nicole considered how he'd ravished her at the house party, and how much fun they'd had at the mill the night before. "*Sweet*. Yep. First word I think of when I consider the man."

Jodie acted far too prim for how much of a party animal she'd been back in the day. "Oh, he's pretty enough."

Cyndi smirked. "*Pretty?* The boy is damn hot, and you know it, Jo. I bet he knows how to—"

"Okay, no more," Nicole interrupted before they dove into territory she had no interest in sharing. "You've done your sisterly duty and warned me off the big bad. This conversation is over."

"He's going to break your heart. Never taking care of anyone but himself—"

"—and he's not done the best job at that *either*."

"*Enough*." Nic took a deep breath. "I'm going out with him. I love you both, but you need to back off and let me make the decisions about my life."

"Well, that's not fair," Jodie said, shocked to the core. "If we can't run our little sister's life, who can we boss around?"

Nicole grabbed another muffin off the plate. "That's what you have husbands for. Go make *their* lives miserable."

The three of them smiled at each other. No hard feelings because it had all been said and done out of love, and Nicole knew that.

Although, with the questions she'd already had about her and Troy's relationship, the conversation had given her a couple more things to think about.

One thing she knew—she refused to let extra doubts slip in without solid reason. She'd caught herself defending him to the terrible twosome. Now she had to make sure she let him defend himself when push came to shove.

Which meant asking a few pointed questions over the next while.

TROY CAUGHT himself whistling as he worked. It was a glorious morning. Sun streamed in the open garage doors, the air was fresh and clean, and there were only a few jobs to take care of. He and Len were in the shop more to deal with any tourist emergencies that might show up.

Len folded his arms over his chest as he stopped beside the toolbox Troy had completely emptied out onto the floor. "You going to do that all day?" he demanded.

"Nah, I'll be done this one in about half an hour. The other two won't take as long, since they—"

"Not the toolbox, *ass*. The noise." Len glared menacingly. "It's like being stuck in a tree full of love-struck birds."

Troy snickered. "What've you got against our fine feathered friends? The bluebird of happiness shit on your Cheerios this morning, bro?"

Len glared harder.

Troy pursed his lips and dove into the most annoying, perky tune he could think of.

"You're such a jerk," Len muttered, but he smiled as he leaned over and grabbed a square plastic container from the mess on the floor.

An industrial-size container of earplugs.

Brilliant. Troy laughed. "My musical talent thanks you for the vote of confidence."

His brother tossed the container at him. "You're more annoying than usual this morning."

"Just in a good mood." He had a girlfriend. Nic was his *girlfriend.*

God, he'd gone off the fucking deep end, but he couldn't stop grinning.

Len shook his head. "Nope. *Good mood* is you after winning a poker game, or pulling a fast one on Clay. Today you're cheerful enough to be nauseating." He looked Troy over. "I heard about Nic."

Of course he had.

Troy grinned. "Gossip chain did its job. Last night or this morning?"

"Last night."

"And...?" Not that he expected Len to be very verbose about what he thought.

His brother hesitated. "She's nice. But you're going to go deaf."

Troy snorted. "Good thing we buy earplugs by the crateful."

Len nodded, but he seemed to have something more he wanted to say, so Troy waited in silence, turning away to deal with a few tools. Checking ratchets and pliers for soundness before putting them back into their places in the massive tool chest.

"You serious about her?" Len asked.

"We just started dating," Troy pointed out with only a twinge of guilt at the underlying lie. Also, he wasn't about to admit to the "this is serious enough we said the word baby" commitment he'd basically given Nic.

Yeah, he was lying his ass off about so many things...

His brother made a low noise.

Tension eased, and Troy laughed. "Was that a 'go you' or a 'give up' grunt? I'm a little slow at Len-speak today."

Len wandered to the toolbox and rested an arm on top.

He looked Troy over as he chewed the inside of his cheek. Troy was ready to give up when his brother finally spit it out. "You should get serious about her. She makes you happy."

"I'm always happy."

A rude snort escaped Len. "You fake it well."

"Fuck off."

Len smiled, the bright expression fading rapidly. "I mean it, Troy. I know you have fun, but fun isn't the same as happy."

"Taking up counseling on the side?" Troy taunted.

"Learning from my mistakes," Len said softly. "Talk to her. Women need you to tell them how you feel and stuff. I nearly lost Janey because of that."

"Nic knows how I feel."

Len shrugged. "Didn't say you'd make the same mistake I did. You'll make your own." His brother shrugged. "You like to be unique. Show-off."

A jab in the gut.

Troy pretended to preen. "That's me. Mr. Show-off."

Len wandered away, his unasked-for advice such as it was delivered. Troy went back to sorting tools, but with that one careless comment, his light mood had turned sour.

The irony of it? The only reason Troy had *ever* sought the spotlight was for his family.

When their mom had died, each of the brothers had found different ways to cope. Not only with losing her, but with how their dad had vanished into the comfort of an alcoholic haze.

Len had gone quiet, and the coyotes had closed in, sensing easy prey. Troy had stepped in the only way he could, turning attention on himself. He'd used his rising sports ability and popularity to draw attention away from his brother. He'd helped the only way a fourteen-year-old boy possibly could, but in the end, him being a show-off had given Len the solace he'd so desperately needed.

When Mitch rebelled it had been tougher. Then, instead of stepping in himself, Troy had sweet-talked one after another of the senior girls into offering to tutor Mitch. It had been a long shot, but it turned out pretty faces and a soft touch got Mitch through enough of his studies to graduate.

His little sister and big brother had pretty much needed the same thing—attention. Katy loved for him to drop in and chat, even for a little while, and Clay... Heck, he'd worked himself like a dog trying desperately to keep the garage up and running, never knowing for sure if it was going to work.

But whenever Troy interrupted, needing something, Clay would light up. Helping his little brother was something he *knew* he could do, whether it was giving him advice, or ordering him around, or driving him places.

The ensuing teasing had annoyed him to no end, but Troy had deliberately failed his driver's test three times in a row just to have a way to make Clay happy.

Screw it. Troy knew *plenty* about taking care of people. He didn't need to give anyone a detailed list about what he'd done in the past. What he did in the future was more important.

And what he was going to do was sweep sweet Nicole Adams off her fucking feet.

As if thinking of her had conjured her, Nicole appeared in the doorway opening, her dark hair swinging as she sauntered into the garage.

"You need a tune-up, sweetheart? Because I'm all yours," Troy offered, walking to meet her.

Bright eyes flashed. "I do like a man who's good with his hands."

Troy caught the back of her neck, pulling her close to draw their bodies into contact as he kissed her.

Nic slipped her hands around him, melting into his embrace. Her willing surrender sweetened the connection, and Troy let her go reluctantly, leaning their foreheads together as he smiled down at her.

"Good to see you."

"I'm not bothering you?"

"Nope." He slipped an arm around her waist and brought her into the shop. "Just you and me and Len here today."

She glanced around, waving as she spotted his brother. "Hey, Len."

Len raised his head from where he was leaning over an open car hood. "Nicole."

"How's Janey?"

His face lit up. "Awesome."

"Good to hear. She asked me over for a barbecue sometime. Oh, and I promised her and Katy I'd set up better accounting systems for them."

"Food is good, but you're really going to help Katy with numbers?" Len grinned. "Glutton for punishment."

"Don't worry, automation is the key."

"Still numbers," Len pointed out. "You can do them in your sleep. Katy and Janey can't."

"Enough," Troy interrupted with a laugh. "Stop flirting with my girlfriend."

Len and Nicole looked at him as if he were out of his mind.

"*Flirting?*" she demanded. "In what universe?"

"He's talking numbers. I know how that turns you on, babe."

"Good grief," Nic muttered as Len laughed then went back to work. She poked Troy in the side. "Turkey."

"It's true," he teased. "I've seen you get all breathless discussing *bottom* lines and *assets*."

He squeezed her butt cheek as he spoke, and she squeaked before slamming her lips together. When a quick glance showed Len wasn't paying attention, she shook a finger at Troy. "Play nice."

"I always do," he promised

She wandered at his side. "You want me to stop bothering you?"

"Hell, no. This isn't rocket science." He led her to his next job, clearing a spot in the counter close to the car then lifting her onto it. "Here. Best seat in the house."

"My hero."

Troy looked her over, appreciating the view. The slope of her breasts rose smoothly behind the worn fabric of her favourite T-shirt. He glanced a second time—the minx wasn't wearing a bra, her soft, bitable nipples clearly pressing against the fabric.

It took him a moment to get himself under control before hauling open the hood and staring blindly into the dark depths trying to remember what came next. "How was your morning?"

"Peachy keen."

Uh-oh. That didn't sound good. "Ominous."

"No, not really. Except...my sisters dropped by."

Ha. Now her pensive mood made sense. "Older and wiser coming to warn you off?"

Bright eyes looked him over as she chewed her lower lip. "...sort of?"

"Did it work?"

Nic shook her head. "They'll hate this, but no. I'll make my own decisions."

She went silent even though the topic didn't seem finished. Obviously something had been said that morning that had gotten her thinking. Troy gave her some room. She'd spill the beans soon enough.

In the meantime...

"You going to give me a hand?"

She frowned, an adorable crease forming between her eyes. "On the..." she shook a hand at the car "...thingy?"

"Tune-up. Yeah. Why not? Or are you afraid to get your hands dirty?"

Nic folded her arms over her chest. "Yeah, right. I'm shaking in my runners."

He held out the wrench. "It's only fair. If I'm going to teach Dale how to do an oil change, I'd better make sure you know a little more than him."

Her eyes gleamed as she popped off the counter and joined him at the car. "Oh, that's brilliant. He's going to be so disappointed when he tries to unsuccessfully one-up me."

Just as competitive as his family. Troy grinned and started his impromptu lesson.

It took over an hour, working together easily, occasionally bumping shoulders. It wasn't about getting hot and heavy, but spending time together. Troy enjoyed himself a lot, especially since Nic seemed to get into it as well.

"You're good at this," Nic said once she'd finished positioning a new air filter, wiping her hands on the soft cloth he'd offered. "I'd need a bit of a reminder to do that all over again, but it wasn't that bad."

"I've done a million tune-ups. You tend to get good after a while."

"Yeah, but it's more than that. You're a good teacher." She handed back the cloth, tilting her head to one side, curiosity written on her face. "You like working here? Doing all the garage stuff?"

He hesitated, wanting to tell her the truth, but his brother was undoubtedly within earshot.

Sure enough, Len's big frame shifted into sight as he moved across the floor to grab something off a shelf.

Troy deliberately offered a nonchalant shrug. "Sure. Work's not bad, other than having to put up with boring old coworkers with no sense of humour—*hey!*"

Len had wandered close enough that his bulky shoulder knocked into Troy and sent him staggering forward, fighting for balance.

"Oops, sorry."

Nicole snickered.

It was impossible to get mad at his brother. Troy met Len's gaze squarely, and his amusement reflected back.

Len stopped as if he meant to stay for a while. "You looking for a part-time job here at the shop?" he tossed Nic's direction.

"Nah. Just bragging rights to Tune-Up Goddess status," she told him. She leaned back on the counter. "If I can convince Maxwell Kent to sell me the '93 Ford Mustang sitting in his back forty I've been teasing him about forever, I'll get you guys to make sure she's roadworthy."

Troy whistled. They'd all had their eye on it at one time or another. It was a gorgeous vehicle. "I know that car. The convertible?"

Nic nodded.

"Max said he'd never sell. That was his son's car." Len raised a brow.

She folded her arms. "Still going to buy it if I can. I'll wear him down."

Len chuckled. "I bet you will."

"It's a sin to let that car molder in a field," Nic insisted.

"Good luck. It would be a great car," Len offered before turning to Troy. "I'm heading home for lunch. Call me?"

"If there's an emergency. Fine," Troy agreed.

"You can take off early once I'm back," Len offered in return, heading toward the door. "Oh. By the way…"

Troy paused in the middle of pulling Nic into his arms, turning her so her back rested against his chest and they faced his brother. "What?"

"You're a brat," Len pronounced. "That ringtone you put on Clay's phone?"

A soft laugh escaped. "Yeah? Did Clay figure it out?"

"Sort of." His brother's grin widened. "Maggie and him decided they like the tune. I didn't have the heart to tell him it was a Nine Inch Nails song, and they should check the words."

Nic sucked in a breath. "You didn't…?"

"Hey, as long as they're happy," Troy told Len.

His brother snorted, shaking his head as he waved goodbye and left the garage.

Nicole's shoulders quivered where she leaned against him. "You're so *bad*."

"Hmmm, I'm so good. Don't worry. If there's any *fucking like animals* going on around here, it'll be us," Troy murmured in her ear.

She waited until the door closed completely behind Len before responding.

"Terrible," she complained, drawing in a gulp of air as he caught hold of her earlobe and nipped lightly.

"You love me being terrible," he offered.

She twisted in his arms and lifted her lips for a kiss.

Sunlight streaked through the open overhead door, lying in stripes across the concrete floor of the shop. The warm summer breeze carried the scent of flowers into the more familiar oil and gas aromas. Familiar, and yet a trap he didn't think he could ever escape.

The sweet kisses from Nic's lips distracted him from the things he couldn't change. And in her arms, he didn't really care. Being there—at that moment—was one thing he didn't want to change.

Troy Thompson liked having a girlfriend.

"Nicole?"

"I'm in here. Back room, on the right," Nicole called in answer.

Laurel poked her head around the corner a moment later, one brow rising. "Localized tornado?"

Nicole picked another T-shirt from the pile on her bed, folding it efficiently as she offered an explanation for the clothing scattered everywhere. "I'm frustrated, and when I'm frustrated I clean. In this case, my closet."

"Great. If you need more material when you're done, you're welcome to come to my place and go through my things," Laurel offered.

"You might not like my methods," Nicole warned, pointing to the stack piled haphazardly against the far wall. "That mess is headed to the thrift shop, if you want to bag it up. Anything you want to keep, it's yours."

Laurel stepped over a pile of shoes and set to work willingly. "Why so frustrated? Troy?"

"No. Well, *yes*, although it's not him." Not completely.

They'd been officially dating for over a week, and for

some stupid reason, regular sex had not yet resumed its place on their dating roster. She wasn't jumping up and down in excitement about that detail.

Nicole balled up another reject shirt and threw it at the discard pile with more energy than needed. It made no sense. She was willing, they were good together, but for whatever reason, Troy was being an *ass* and keeping things on a slow burn.

It was probably melodramatic to complain that her skin itched, but she was so—*achy*. She hated the word horny, but if the urge to get down and dirty fit...

Gahhhh. She was doing it again. Obsessing over sex when she was supposed to be focusing on whether they could be a forever couple or not. *Great.*

Not boring, though, her brain muttered.

This time she didn't tell herself to shut up; she was too confused to fight it.

"You guys have fun at the drive-in last night?" Laurel asked, drawing her back to the real world.

"Yeah. Movie was okay. And he went with me to the wreckers before to find a replacement part for my trunk lock."

"*Ooooh*, a trip to the wreckers." Laurel batted her lashes rapidly, clutching her hands over her chest like a storybook heroine. "So *romantic*."

"Shut up." Nicole laughed. "It was great. We had fun wandering around, grabbing bits and pieces from all the old vehicles. Troy knew a ton of people who needed things, so we came out with a trunk full of crazy stuff to pass on to others."

Laurel settled on the edge of the bed. "Sounds like a great time. Dating is going well then."

"Yeah..."

It was true. She wasn't even sure why she felt so edgy. It wasn't as if she was being completely cock-blocked. They'd kissed and fooled around plenty. Troy was damn generous when it came to handing her orgasms, but actual sex?

She was about to explode from frustration, but she wasn't sure she wanted to share her acutely sexual problem with Laurel, no matter how hard they'd clicked as friends.

Fortunately... *Unfortunately?* The no-sex issue wasn't the only thing she had to complain about. Nicole took a deep breath and let Laurel have it. "My family is driving me nuts."

"That's what family does."

"This is beyond typical. *Nutsier?* Think more annoying than usual. Damn them for their well-intentioned curiosity and maddening advice."

"Ahh, yes." Laurel folded another item then tucked it into the bag she was filling. "But...I thought you said your family likes Troy."

A heavy sigh escaped her. "Oh, they like him. *Everyone* likes him. They just don't think he's more than a pretty face and a good time waiting to happen."

"He's held a steady job at the garage for over seven years. What does he need to do to prove he's grown up?" Laurel demanded.

Nicole was at a loss for a better answer. "I have no idea. My brother-in-law went in and took his oil-changing lesson from Troy, and I was sure that would make a good impression, but he just kind of grunted and told me to be careful not to get hurt."

Her friend sighed heavily. "Troy can't win them over, can he?"

"Other than magically turning into a buttoned-up professor, I don't see how."

Laurel went strangely quiet for a moment. "Umm, even that's not a guarantee of not breaking your heart. Why does he have to be serious?"

Maybe that was the trouble. Nic had been one hundred percent on Team Serious when she'd started…

"I…like Troy," she confessed.

"D-uh. I hope so." Laurel flashed her a smile. "You're going out with him. Liking him makes that work better."

Nicole dropped onto the mattress across from her friend. "No, I mean, I *really* like him. I guess I always have, but I'd always put him into a fun-times box and never thought he could be more."

"Fucking friends, not forever soul mates?"

Nicole choked on her own spit. "Will you *stop* that?"

"Sorry," Laurel said without a blush. "But seriously, you don't expect me to believe you're not sleeping with him. You two were—" She slammed to a stop before shaking her head. "Nope. I won't go there. Suffice to say, you didn't seem to have any chemistry issues…"

Ha. They were the only couple she knew to have screwed around before they started officially dating *then* go virginal. "The chemistry is there, but the lab seems to be closed," she confessed.

It took Laurel a split second to parse that out, her eyes widening. "Since *when*?"

"Since we started dating, damnabbit."

Laurel's lips twitched. "Ix-nay on that as a swear substitute, although I thoroughly accept the need to swear. I'm in shock."

"I'm in worse than shock," Nicole complained. "Although, if you don't like talking about sex, we can stop."

Her friend shrugged. "Hardly necessary. Being raised in the church doesn't mean I'm ignorant about sex. In fact, I've heard all sorts of twisted things under the guise of 'confessing our sins and evil desires'."

"*Ewwww*, thank you for that."

"No prob," Laurel said. "But since *I* have no sex life—by choice, I might add—let's go back to talking about *your* no sex life, since it seems to not make sense."

"Maybe he's just..." Nope. "Or maybe it's..." Nope, not that either. Nicole stared at the wall.

"No way. You haven't even *asked*? Or better yet, just straight-out seduced him?" Laurel shook her head before rummaging in the bag of discarded clothing and pulling out a tank top. "Here, wear that, with no bra, and tell me he keeps his dick in his pants."

Nicole was dying, gasping for air. The longer Laurel went on, the harder it got to breathe. "What the hell kind of church-going upbringing did you have, young lady?"

"Trust me, this isn't about my upbringing. It's a very solid research education conducted online during college. But enough about me." Laurel shoved the shirt into her hands.

Nicole took one final suck of air to stop herself from falling over before checking out the shirt with horror. "I've had this thing since junior high. It barely covers my ta-tas."

"I bet your ta-tas look awesome barely covered with it. That's the point. And now..." Laurel leaned back on the pillow propped against the wall "...riddle me this. You asked if I was okay talking about sex."

"Yeah?"

Her friend gave her that one-brow-raised expression. "Have you asked Troy why you're not having sex?"

Nicole opened her mouth. Closed it.

"Gee, why not?"

"You're annoying, did you know that?" Nicole demanded.

"Yup." Laurel stared straight at her. "Well, hon, in my opinion, if you're not fucking, you *should* be talking."

"One or the other, is that it?"

"Both at the same time if he's talented, I suppose. I hear that can be hot."

"You're making me crazy," Nicole warned.

"Good. That means we've reached the friends-who-hug stage of the game. Yes?"

Nicole laughed. "Yeah. Okay, you're right. I need to ask him why, or encourage him to spill the beans, or whatever."

Laurel's soft smile shone like a blessing. "Talking is good."

"Fucking is good too," Nicole muttered. "But yeah, he's a pretty typical guy. Getting him to put two words together about anything serious... It's not happening."

"Hard to know if this is going to work if you're just dancing along like you did before. Not that being happy and having fun is wrong," she insisted. "I just mean you need to talk while you're having fun, to make sure you're headed in the same direction."

Nicole's head swam with ideas, but she felt way better for sharing with someone instead of stewing in her own misery. "You *are* awesome," she told Laurel, rounding the bed to offer a hug.

Laurel popped to her feet. "No prob."

They were still squeezing each other tight when a low rumble hit from the doorway. "I have nothing against girl-on-girl action, but hands off, Sitko. That's *my* girlfriend—"

Oh my *God*. Nicole twirled to face Troy. "It's not—"

Laurel laughed softly in the background as Nicole found herself hauled into his arms and kissed breathless. By the time he let her up for air, her friend had vanished, the bag of charity clothes with her.

Except for the far-too-small top Laurel had left in plain sight on the edge of the bed. Brat.

Nicole clung to Troy's leather-clad shoulders. "There was nothing going on, you *turkey*."

"I know that," Troy said. "I like Laurel. She makes you happy."

Even a quick mental review of the afternoon visit proved that was true. Nicole looked Troy over more closely. "Going somewhere?"

"Yeah, for a ride with you." He tilted his head toward the door. "Come on, I brought a spare helmet. The sky is clear and it's a beautiful day. Let's not waste it."

HE'D BEEN BIDING his time...

No.

He'd been working his ass off...

No.

Troy let loose a mental sigh as he admitted the truth, at least to himself.

He'd been using every bit of strength he had to keep from jumping Nicole. *And* he'd been trying his best to figure out what in the hell it would take to impress the people important to Nic without up and magically turning into someone else.

At that moment, with Nicole tucked up against his back, her arms around his waist, life was just about perfect. Connected like this, racing down the highway, he got to savour the warmth transferring from her thighs to his without worrying about how he was going to screw up by not being serious enough.

Avoiding topics he didn't want to go into was getting tougher all the time, and he felt like the stupidest shit.

He'd spent the past twelve years impressing people and making them like him, and now, when it was important? Bullshit on him having any moves.

The moments they were alone things were great. Except for avoiding sex, the idea for which he was equal parts proud of and ready to shoot himself in the head for.

He really was trying to make sure they had something *more* than sex going on, but the fact they didn't have sex going on at the same time was bugging the hell out of both of them.

They were screwed. Neither of them knew how to do this grow-up-and-move-on thing. Or at least he sure didn't.

Nicole squeezed him tight then pointed to the side. He followed the line of her arm, turning down the side road when he spotted her target.

Maxwell Kent's convertible.

He pulled to a stop beside her, waiting for Nicole to get off the bike before joining her as she paced around the vehicle. "She's a beauty," he said.

"This car makes me think dirty thoughts," Nic confessed. "Long, slow make-out sessions in the summer sunshine. The scent of Coppertone sunscreen. Driving home with the top down after a lazy trip down the river."

"Parking on the ridge and watching the stars wink into view over the Rockies..."

Nic flashed a smile at him. "God, so much fun." She stepped forward, trailing her fingers over the dusty blue paint. Her bright smile faded.

"What's wrong?" he asked softly. He leaned across the hood, wondering why her fire had extinguished so fast.

She glanced up, smile back in place.

Absolutely fake.

"*Nic...*" he warned.

An enormous sigh escaped her, but she lifted her gaze to his. "Buy me a drink, and I'll tell you my troubles, sailor."

He worried the entire way to the nearest watering hole. The tiny village was no more than a gas station with an attached café, the sole survivor of a handful of decrepit buildings that had risen around the intersection of two seldom-traveled secondary highways.

They walked with linked fingers into the shop. A small bell overhead rang briefly then cut out with a static-filled *bleep*. Troy guided her to a bench seat before grabbing them two Cokes from the bored-out-of-her-skull teenaged girl manning the counter.

Nic poured her drink into a glass then focused all her attention on picking at the label on the empty plastic bottle.

"Once more with feeling," Troy ordered, speaking quietly but firmly. "You were having a ball talking about that car then suddenly you went cold. What the hell happened?"

She lifted her eyes to meet his. "All this while I've been going on about wanting to move forward. Leave behind my impulsive ways, and dive into being a real adult. That car?" She shook her head. "About as childish as I could get."

"Bullshit." His response was instant.

"Right. I can see it now. Top rolled down, wind whipping through my hair as I cruise down the highway, baby seat strapped in the back—" She made a rude noise.

"Why not?" Troy demanded. "It's a car, not a fucking pogo stick."

"Because responsible adults don't spend their time and energy on stupid toys that aren't necessary. I don't need that car."

"But you want that car," Troy pointed out. "The idea makes you happy. There's nothing wrong with that. You should do more things that make you happy."

"No, I should do more things that help me reach my goals," Nic corrected.

"And your goal is to be miserable?"

"Stop being an ass," she snapped. "Yes, I like the car, but it's never going to happen because buying it isn't being responsible."

He'd had enough. "For fuck's sake. There's no reason you can't have the 'Stang. I'll trade in my damn truck for a fucking minivan if that's what we need down the road."

Tick.

Tick.

Tick.

The old-fashioned cuckoo clock on the wall and the tinny sound of music from behind the cook-station doors seemed loud in the silence that rolled in.

He couldn't quite believe what had just come out of his mouth.

Neither could Nic from the way her jaw hung partially open.

They stared at each other for a moment before she got herself together faster than him. "*Really.*"

It wasn't what she said, but how, and the chin jut that accompanied it. Challenging him.

"You don't have to be boring to be responsible," he repeated. "You don't have to change who you are to move on to the next stage of life."

Her eyes narrowed. "Oh, don't even try to hand me that

line. Considering that ever since we officially started going out, the one thing we did well, sex—"

She jerked to a stop, cheeks flushed as the waitress girl wandered past, wiping down the table to their right.

As they waited in silence for her to move out of earshot, something miraculous occurred. For the second time that month, Troy had an epiphany.

The first time, he'd realized they were right together. Now he realized it with even more certainty.

They were right together. Not two other people who acted differently. Who spent their days doing different things. He'd been wrong to try to impress anyone but her with anything but his real self. And wrong for holding off on the physical side of things.

Enough. Time to get real. "The only bullshit is the fact I haven't been inside you for too damn long. Not fucking around with you *sucks*."

He might have said it a tad too loud, but she pressed her lips together to hide her smile even as she glanced to see if he'd been overheard. "Jeez. You want to put it out in a meme? Hashtag that sentiment for everyone to see?" she murmured.

"*Hashtag fuck you raw?* It has trending potential."

She snorted. "God, you're terrible." Nic looked him over, her gaze lingering on his hands and torso as a full-out smile took possession of her lips. "So. You plan on doing this fucking today, tomorrow or next week?"

He picked up his glass and drained the rest of it in one shot, waiting impatiently until she finished the remainder of her drink. Before she could say another word he herded her out of the booth, out of the café, and toward his bike.

"In a hurry?" she asked as he forced her helmet into her hands.

"Damn straight. Unless you want me to fuck you right here in the parking lot."

He wasn't joking, and she knew it. A heavy pulse race to life at the base of her throat.

Hmmmm. "Tempted, baby?"

"We've never done that. How do you have sex on a bike?" she murmured, the words tight with desire.

Troy swore softly, taking over doing up her chinstrap since her hands hung uselessly at her sides. "Hard. Fast. Now get on behind me before I change my mind and give you a demonstration you won't forget in a hurry."

He had the urge to put her over the leather seat and follow through with his threat, especially since it wasn't fear he'd seen in her eyes.

Curiosity. Anticipation—that's what was on her mind, which proved all over again what he'd told himself before going off on some misguided celibacy path.

Nicole Adams was fucking perfect for him.

She liked her sex wild and nearly out of control, and her lover bossy as hell. Him to a T, especially after days of being tormented to a feverish pitch by his good intentions and bad timing.

Hell, jerking off in the mornings had barely blunted the edge.

She curled up behind him, wrapping her arms around his body and sealing her torso to his an instant before he floored it, laying rubber behind in the parking lot as he accelerated out the exit and back onto the highway.

Nicole tugged at his T-shirt, easing her hand under the edge as soon as she could to drag her nails over his abdomen.

His cock hardened further, a curse escaping his lips as the impossibility of adjusting to a less painful position registered. But he didn't want her to stop either, the warmth of her palm driving him wild, the sheer cheekiness of her actions as she reached up and dragged the nail over his nipple...

Screw making it back to town. Troy pulled off the side of the road onto a narrow gravel trail on completely unknown land. It led toward a barn, the old structure set far off from the highway and nowhere near any other outbuildings. Abandoned, but still somewhat out of eyeshot from the main highway.

He came to a stop on the north side of the building, glancing quickly in all directions, pleased to see what appeared to be endless farmers' fields.

Nicole dismounted, pulling off her helmet, lips twisting. "You lost?"

"I know exactly where I am," he insisted grabbing the helmet from her and tossing it to the ground by the front tire. "Five minutes from making you scream."

She pressed her hands to his chest as he dragged her into his arms, sliding upward until she could hook her fingers together behind his neck. "Oh, really?"

He waited just long enough to let her finish speaking before kissing her as if he were starving. Lips connecting as he reached down and caught hold of her hips, lifting her in the air. She wrapped her legs around him, and he stepped toward the barn, pressing her against it. He kept one arm between her upper back and the rough wood, the other hand slipping between them to undo his jeans and zipper.

Hands on automatic, he focused on her lips, her taste welling through him. It had been too damn long since they'd been together, and he simply couldn't wait.

He nipped at the soft spot where her shoulder met her neck, and Nicole gasped in pleasure, body arching toward him.

"I'm going to fuck you right here," he warned.

"Yes."

The word came out with another gasp as he nipped her earlobe. Troy was going to lose his ever-loving mind. Next time he'd have the ability to do more than act like some crazed animal.

But he was no asshole.

"You ready for me?" He jerked aside the gusset of her underwear, trailing his fingers through her warmth. "Jeez, woman. You're wet. You like the idea of being fucked against the side of a barn, don't you?"

"*Yes.*"

Nicole caught his mouth with hers, biting his lower lip hard enough he tasted blood. He didn't fucking care—everything was a blur as he shoved his hand into his pocket and grabbed a condom, dragging it over his aching cock a split second before he lined up with her sex.

Somehow Troy regained his control for long enough to pause and look her in the eye. She wanted this. He *needed* it like an addict needed his next hit.

She stared back, eyes gone hazy with lust. He drove home in one stroke.

Her eyes widened, lips opening on a moan. "*Troy.*"

"God, you feel so good around me."

Her breath fluttered out as she tightened her thighs around him. "You feel so good inside me."

Then the minx smiled, mischief drifting in that he didn't understand for a split-second until he felt her squeeze, body gripping him like a fist. "*Fuck.*"

Her smile widened. "Yes."

He eased back his hips, slower than he thought possible, taking in the sensation of hot, wet paradise until he nearly escaped her body. Pausing long enough to make her anticipate what he'd do next.

Slow. Slower than she'd expected. Slower than expected considering the urgent desire commanding him to thrust.

Slow enough that when their bodies met it was as if he had forced all the air out of her. A sweet sigh of satisfaction floated past him on the warm afternoon air.

Again. A drag back, pressure forward. Vicious pleasure rippled up his spine and made his head spin.

His patience and control lasted a dozen strokes before he could take it no longer. Troy slipped a hand between them, placing his thumb over her clit to urge her along. All it took was that simple touch, and she jerked in his arms, fingernails digging into his shoulders.

"*Yessssss.*"

Hell, yeah. And it was all systems go—

Forget finesse, forget trying to torment her to further pleasure. Troy rocked faster and faster, driving his cock deep as Nic continued to moan and cry out. Stars floated in front of his eyes as he gasped for air. Urgent need unraveled, starting at the base of his spine before it propelled through his entire system.

He was the center of an explosion, the detonation escaping through his cock and leaving him wasted.

And very *very* eager to do it all over again.

His head was still spinning as he realized Nicole was dancing kisses over his face. Along his jawline, his cheeks. Whispering contented words the entire time.

Somehow he had managed to keep his arm in place, protecting her from the wood, although—*damn it.*

"You're gonna have bruises tomorrow," he muttered, stroking a hand over her hip where he'd clutched her at the end, far too powerfully for her fair skin.

She kissed him, gentle, lips curled into a smile. "I don't mind."

He was a bastard, but there was not much he could do at this point. "I don't want to leave you."

A chuckle escaped her. "It's going to get pretty tiring holding me up all night. Maybe we should go back to my place. Try this again on a mattress..."

A wave of satisfaction and relief hit nearly as hard as his climax had. "No arguments from me. Unless you're pissed I made you wait and then lost it against the side of a damn barn."

She stroked the rough stubble on his cheek. "I'm stubborn, not stupid. I'll admit it. I still don't know what we're doing, but I like you, Troy Thompson. I like you the way you are—impulsive, and strong, and *oh my God* sexy." She brushed her lips over his. "Come on. Take me home."

CHAPTER 13

Night and day difference.

They'd turned a page, and suddenly all the things she'd loved about spending time with Troy before they'd became a couple were back, while stretching their boundaries into new territory.

Troy would pick her up after work, and they'd head off to do typical summer things like hitting the local hangout by the river. Playing around on the rope swing that hung under the railway bridge, and splashing down into the refreshing water. Or sitting in lawn chairs with their friends and shooting the breeze until the stars made an appearance. At which point they'd head out and end up somewhere, hip deep in sex.

They hadn't set a deadline on whatever this was they were doing, but slowly, steadily, the doubts she'd had about him were fading. Maybe he'd been footloose before, but so had she.

Spending time together wasn't earth-shattering, but it was enjoyable, and easy, and right.

Only two uncomfortable issues remained. Kids—i.e.,

was Troy really interested? And her family's ongoing disapproval.

Whenever they were around her family, it was clear the entire Adams Collective was waiting with bated breath for the relationship to fall apart so she could move on to better pastures. Their lack of faith was frustrating on so many levels.

Although Mike seemed to have calmed down somewhat. At least Troy hadn't reported any middle-of-the-night death threats.

Still, she worked to reassure them all even as she waded through unfamiliar waters. She spent time with her sisters and their families, with or without Troy, and tried to ignore the annoying.

It was hard to ignore at times.

Nicole had joined her parents for Sunday-morning breakfast, and everything had been going great until the program froze on the same damn topic as before.

"I ran into Chase at the grocery store yesterday," her mom informed her.

"I hope you didn't hurt him too much," Nicole said, completely straight-faced.

Her mother blinked, considered, then rolled her eyes.

Nicole was sure she had the only mother on earth who rolled her eyes.

"He's settling into town nicely," her mom continued, "but he'd love a tour of the local hiking trails."

"Really."

"He's free this afternoon."

Good grief. "That's nice. Have fun."

"What...?" Her mother laughed. "Oh, stop kidding around. You need to take him."

"I'm busy, Mom."

Her dad frowned as he boomed over the table, "Too busy to be neighbourly to newcomers? That's not very nice, Nicole."

"Neither is trying to set me up with someone when Mom knows I'm already dating someone else," Nicole answered as pleasantly as possible.

Her dad looked thoroughly confused. "Who are you dating?" He glanced at Darlene. "I thought you said the Thompson boy was out of the picture."

"Why would you think that?" Nicole demanded.

Her mother looked uncomfortable. "The girls said it was only a matter of time, and—"

"He's not very grounded," her dad announced loudly. "Good boy, but not much more there than what you see. No ambition. You should move on. Let him go, and find someone who's got what it takes."

The sound of someone clearing his throat broke through the tension. All three of them whirled to face the back entrance, and Nicole's heart plummeted. Troy stood in the doorway, his patented happy-go-lucky grin firmly in place.

He held a box in his hands, and as if it wasn't the most awkward moment ever, he strode forward to offer it to Nicole's mom. "My sister's garden is going great guns. She sent over some of the early harvest."

Darlene slipped into recovery mode, rushing from the table and directing Troy where to put the box. Gushing over the contents even as she tossed meaningful looks over Troy's shoulder at Brian, and condemning ones at Nicole.

Nope. It wasn't *her* fault her parents had behaved like asses. And it wasn't as if she'd known Troy was coming over. She wouldn't have wished that bullshit on anyone, especially not him.

They escaped shortly after, Troy tucking her into his

truck and driving them away. She tried to figure out the best way to apologize when she wasn't sure how much he'd overheard...

Before she could come up with a solution, he broke the silence. "Katy asked if we could come over early to help set up for the barbecue. You okay if we head over there now?"

"No problem. Glad to help."

He caught her fingers in his, resting their joined hands on her thigh. Humming softly—a light, easy tune. The mood was comfortable and right, a stark contrast to the awkwardness of only moments earlier.

She laid her head against his shoulder and wondered how he did that so quickly—turned a stressful situation into something far less volatile.

By the afternoon, all the Thompsons had showed up at the gathering except for Maggie, Clay's fiancée, who was out of town visiting her parents, and Anna, who was on shift. Nicole caught herself gazing after Troy as something nagged at her. She knew something was off but couldn't define it enough to vocalize it.

The guys and Janey took off for some pick-up football after the meal, leaving Nicole and Katy with a sleeping Tanner. The little guy was so cute, curled up against Katy's chest, his dark curls hanging over his forehead.

Nicole tilted her chair back and stared into the sky, content to watch the game from the sidelines as she tried to unscramble the uneasiness in her soul.

The Thompsons had welcomed her in, no problem. Why couldn't her family do the same for Troy? As a couple they seemed to be closing in on something amazing, but it scared her to see her family hesitating. More than hesitating—downright dismissive of what she was experiencing.

She let her gaze drift to where the guys and Janey

were tossing the football between them. Troy's firm muscles flexed as he stole the ball from Clay and passed it to Janey, laughing easily as Len stepped in to guard her protectively.

Was she that bad a judge of character? What was she missing that her family was worried about?

"Penny for your thoughts," Katy offered.

"Is that still an expression?" Nicole pushed herself back to vertical. "We don't have pennies anymore."

"It sounds wrong to offer nickels."

Nicole snickered.

Katy grinned back. "You're thinking hard about something. Everything okay with you and Troy?"

"We're good." Nicole paused. "I think we're good." She met Katy's gaze. "He *acts* as if we're good."

The other woman snorted. "I figured as much." Katy dragged her fingers through her son's hair, her face softening as she admired him. "I love my brothers, but they have their moments."

"Troy's been great." Oh, damn. What if Katy was going to make negative comments about him? She couldn't take anyone else cutting him down—not after her parents' stupidity earlier in the day. "I'm the one with issues," she insisted.

"You're dating. Things aren't going to go completely smoothly," Katy assured her. "This is the time to figure out each other, only..." She made a face. "Only out of all my brothers? Troy is going to be the least likely to pony up and admit if something is wrong."

"I've never noticed Troy to have any trouble sharing what's on his mind," Nicole offered, thinking back to how many times in the past month he'd astonished her.

"Oh, he's always got plenty to say. Len's the one with a

word quota for the day, but Troy? He can talk for hours and say nothing about himself. Nothing real, at least."

Like on the ride over. Had he heard her parents? Damn her for not asking.

Katy pressed a kiss to Tanner's head before rearranging the toddler more comfortably in her arms. She looked up to meet Nicole's eyes. "When Mom got sick, everything tipped sideways. I was young enough what I remember most are emotions. Like being upset I couldn't have a birthday party —Mom was going through chemo, and she was too ill to bake a cake or organize anything."

"God. You were...ten...when she got sick?"

"Close. Eleven, going on twelve, which for some kids would be old enough to react better, but while I knew Mom couldn't help it, inside, that moment was still all about me."

"Kids don't understand."

"No, and I don't blame myself or anything." Katy stared out at her family, her dad in the middle of the action, laughing loudly. "And so many details are gone, but the emotions? I can remember those clearly, as if bright splashes of colour were tossed over each of us. Dad went black with sorrow. Clay was this dark green—protective and focused on getting stuff done."

Nicole liked the idea of associating colours with emotions. "I can guess Mitch. He went wild. Red?"

"*Bright* red. Especially after I walked into the house and found him bleeding after a fight. God, you should have heard me scream. I thought he was going to die right there in the kitchen."

So many memories. "Mike and I were fourteen. I remember bits of it happening—your mom being sick—but we were all tangled up in our own lives. And what Troy let slip when he was around Mike."

Katy nodded. "Len went pale yellow, nearly invisible."

Which made sense. "And Troy?"

The other woman hesitated. "Part of me wants to say blue, like a clear winter sky. But that's not right, because he was also green, and yellow and red and purple..."

"You've been watching too many musicals."

Katy snorted. "I can't explain it any other way. He was always there, Nic. Not like Clay, making sure I had everything I needed for school, but every time I needed someone around, he was there. He helped me in the kitchen without anyone knowing it, and he flirted with my friends, which smoothed so much teenage drama. And any time tears rolled in, Troy would show up and make me laugh."

He'd always been good at that. It was part of what had attracted Nicole in the first place. His sense of humour. His ability to make her happy—not only in the bedroom.

"So Troy's a rainbow?" Nicole smiled. "It fits. He does brighten up the world."

"I hope he's really doing what makes him happy." Katy jerked her head toward Nicole, panic in her eyes. "I'm not saying *you* don't make him happy—you're awesome. Really. I just...he's complicated, that's all."

"I can agree with that." The man had surprised her too many times for her to argue.

Tanner woke, fussing and wiggling in Katy's lap.

She stood. "I'd better change him before the rest of the crew stops playing and starts looking for dessert."

Curiosity made Nicole ask. "What colour were you, by the way?"

Katy adjusted Tanner on her hip, smiling softly as she paused to answer. "*I* was blue. Sad that Mom was gone, but like most young kids, more focused on the next thing, and the next day."

The conversation on top of everything simply added to the whirling in Nicole's brain. She was still trying to sort things out when the evening came to a close, waving good-byes to everyone before Troy helped her into his truck.

Maybe she didn't have all the answers, but she figured it was as good a time as any. "Want to come over to my place for a while?"

"Sure."

The flash in his eyes was one hundred percent sexual. She had no objections to where they ended the evening, but first, she had an agenda.

She was no longer thinking about their relationship being over, she was thinking how to make it never end. If they were going to do this forever thing, she wanted it all. Him right now, him in the future...

Him of the past.

No matter how tightly capped his history was, Katy's comments combined with a few things he'd said over their time together made Nicole reflect.

She'd always loved figuring out puzzles. She'd just never realized Troy Thompson was the biggest mystery in her life in ways she'd never imagined.

TROY WATCHED with amusement as Nic wandered past him for the third time in two minutes. They'd made it to her house and she'd been pacing ever since. Turning on music, grabbing a drink, adjusting the lights.

"Enough. Quit fidgeting." He caught her by the hand and tugged her off balance, tipping her from her feet into his lap. "I want a kiss."

She lifted her lips willingly enough, warm fingers

curling through his hair as their bodies nestled together. Soft in all the right places, he thought as he settled his hands on her hips and brought her closer.

"Hmmm, you're distracting me," she whispered against his lips.

"You got something else you need to do tonight? Paperwork? Month-end accounts?" Troy pulled back far enough to brush his lips over her cheek.

"I want to talk," she confessed. "And apologize."

Troy had wondered if she'd get around to mentioning her parents' conversation. He planted his feet on the floor and twisted until he could relax back against the couch, all the time keeping her butt firmly positioned in his lap. "Talk, but you're not going anywhere."

Nic draped an arm around his neck, pressing her other palm to his face. "I don't know if you overheard my parents being idiots, and I debated not saying anything in case you hadn't, but you need to know *I'm* very happy with how things are going. Between us, I mean."

"Except for your parents being idiots?"

"Except for that," she agreed. Her head tilted slightly. "They do like you."

"I hear that a lot," Troy deadpanned. "I'm a likable guy." He lowered his gaze to where his hand lay against her thigh, stroking lightly back and forth over the worn denim of her jeans.

"Troy?"

"Hmmm?" He curled his fingers around her leg, lifting until she ended up straddling him. The position put her close enough the heat of her sex sank through the layers between them to tease his cock, and he instinctively rubbed them together.

Nic laughed softly. "One-track mind."

"I'm a healthy male in the prime of life. Additional tracks don't kick in until I turn thirty or something." Troy nuzzled against her neck, breathing in the scent of her skin. Warm and aroused, even if she wanted to talk.

"Bullshit," she murmured. "You're not just a sex machine. You're one of the smartest people I know."

He reached for the buttons on her shirt. "Compliments, now. Well, I might even let you do dirty things to me if this keeps up."

"I'm going to get you to talk to me," she warned even as she stroked his shoulders.

Troy smiled. It was nice to see her relaxed, even if she was determinedly persistent about whatever was on her mind. He opened another button, just enough he could brush his knuckles against the skin showing above the upper edge of her bra. "I propose a game."

"Of course you do." Their eyes met as a smile curled her lips.

"Strip Questions."

Her laughter rolled over him. "For every question I ask, I lose an article of clothing? What kind of game is that?"

"I made it up myself. I think it has potential to become *the* new party game."

He could see the gears turning—probably mentally counting how many items she was wearing before deciding *not enough*.

"Troy...I'm serious. Katy said you're the toughest person to get the truth out of. So prove her wrong, and tell me your secrets, pretty please?"

As much fun as it was to tease, Troy had no objections to helping Nicole deal with whatever was on her mind. Sharing was another part of proving they were right for each other, wasn't it?

Something inside opened a tiny crack—hope rising that maybe, just maybe, he'd get to share some secrets he'd held inside forever. But only if she asked…

He tucked a finger under her chin and tipped her face toward him. "I'll stop mucking around. What's on your mind, baby?"

Nicole adjusted position slightly, forearms resting on his shoulders as she continued to stoke her fingers over his neck and through his hair. "Why *didn't* you go to university?"

Holy shit, she'd asked. "Wow—starting with the big guns."

Her expression softened. "I'm not asking to hurt you, but you turning down that scholarship made no sense."

"They needed me at the garage."

Her nose wrinkled. "Your three brothers and your dad all worked there."

Which was true, but it wasn't the complete story. A dozen people working the shop wouldn't have given Thompson and Sons what they'd really needed back then—

Troy eased open that crack a little further. "Does it change things if I tell you I didn't *want* to play football?"

"At university?"

"Ever." Her forehead creased as she examined him closely. He continued before she could interrupt. "I played because there was a good reason to, and yeah, I was talented enough to help the team, but that's it. Football was a means to an end."

"Okaaaaay." She dragged out the word, but was obviously thinking, not being a smartass. "I never guessed… I thought you enjoyed football. You and Mike had a great team the last two years of high school. I went to all the games"—she made a face—"we all did. The entire family.

We'd end up sitting with your dad, Len, and Katy, eating too many stadium hotdogs."

And every time he'd look into the stands and see his father sitting there, it made playing worthwhile. Memories swirled—

A soft touch on his cheek brought him back. "Troy?"

"Just trying to decide how many old bones to dig up," he admitted.

"This has something to do with football?"

He nodded, frustration rising. "It gets complicated, because it's not only about me, it's about other people and their secrets. Their pain."

She curled her arms around him. "Your dad?"

"Yeah," he acknowledged. "When Mom died, part of Dad did too. He got lost in the bottle for a while, but the year I hit high school, he read some article about the football team. None of my brothers really played—I think Clay had one season before he and Mitch got busy trying to keep the shop from going under while Dad drank. For some reason, though, he saw that flyer and got all excited. He insisted I try out."

"So you did. Even though you weren't interested?"

"*He* was interested, and that was good enough for me." Troy stroked a strand of hair back off her face, tucking it behind her ear. "I hated that training meant I couldn't help as much at the shop, but every time I had a game, he was there, Nic. There, and sober, and so damn proud his son was the star quarterback—it made him come alive for a little while. How could I not put in the effort to make that happen, no matter what it took on my part?"

"Oh, Troy." She patted his chest. "You played for him."

"For the family, because those nights he'd come home and be something like a father. He'd talk to Katy and Len.

He'd help deal with the tougher repair jobs Clay and Mitch were fighting with. He'd be our dad again, at least for a few hours before the misery would catch hold."

She paused to think it through. "It must be a real pain in the ass every time someone pokes you about turning down the scholarship. Or about being a superstar jock." Her eyes widened. "Oh my God, the never-ending conversation about the *throw of the decade*."

Troy laughed. "I didn't *hate* football, but I didn't love it. And my ego is certainly not based around whether or not I can throw a damn pigskin, so I ignore them. I just slap up a wall and it doesn't matter. But, Nic?" He tilted her head so their gazes met straight on. "I don't want to pretend with you."

"I will never again jock-block you." She blinked hard, nose twitching.

There was another issue. "I would hate for my father to find out I played football to keep him from being passed-out stinking drunk the three days a week we had games. All that would do is make him feel guilty."

"That's why you never make a big fuss about not drinking, right? To protect him?"

She and Mike were probably the only people who'd noticed he always abstained. Troy paused before nodding. "And I don't talk about any of this with my brothers—they saw things differently, and that's fine—"

"They thought you were slacking off." She shook her head.

"Hell, maybe I was, a bit," he started, but she interrupted again.

"You were helping in your own way," Nic insisted.

He nodded, stroking her skin again. "Doesn't change the past to tell them everything I did for them that they never knew about. It would just make them feel like crap. Why bother? I'm a big boy. I don't need to be petted and told I'm pretty."

"I promise, I won't say a word. About any of it." Sad understanding shone in her eyes. "Do you ever think about going to university now?"

"They still need me," he said quietly.

"Ignore that for a moment. If you *could* go, what would you take? Advanced mechanics?"

"Teaching. Or coaching."

Her eyes widened. "That's not at all what I expected."

He snorted. "Yeah, I suppose not."

"No, I shouldn't have assumed. Would you teach shop?"

"God, no." The answer came instantly. He smiled sheepishly. "Sorry, but the idea of spending a lifetime surrounded by tires and timing belts makes my skin crawl. I'd prefer to teach phys ed, or maybe go a different route entirely and become a personal trainer."

"That would be a way to use your Golden Boy reputation for good, not evil," she teased gently.

"I liked working out and using my body." His lips twitched. "The experience may as well open a few doors."

Nicole leaned in and kissed him. Soft and slow. Tongues barely touching before she pulled back and started all over again. He let her set the pace, smiling as she fluttered kisses along his jaw and down his neck.

It had been a huge moment for him—sharing like that. Troy might not *need* to be petted, but it didn't mean he objected to some good old-fashioned admiration from Nic. Her opinion mattered, and he trusted her to keep his secrets. He didn't want to think about how much it would hurt if this all fell apart on them, and he lost the chance to be with her.

"I'm not happy with you," she said even as she tugged at his T-shirt.

"Really? Damn, what would you be doing right now if you *were* happy? Because I'm pretty good with the status quo."

She helped him peel the fabric off over his head, her hands instantly returning to caress his chest. "Why did it take until now to have this conversation?"

"Because it wasn't important—"

Fingers pressed over his lips stopped him in his tracks, her frown firmly in position as she glared at him. "No bullshit. You *promised*."

He waited until her fingers loosened, slipping a kiss to her palm before she pulled her hand away. "No bullshit. I'm glad you know, but we're twenty-six years old, Nic. What happened nine, ten years ago is part of what got us to this point, but what's here and now is what matters."

She nodded decisively. "Agreed."

Then her eyes widened as he slid his hands under her shirt, and she moaned as he undid her bra and pushed aside the fabric to cover her naked breasts with his palms.

"Talking time is over," he murmured against her lips. "I want you."

HER MIND WAS STILL TRYING to catch up, but now it was the touch of his hands on her body that made it impossible to focus. Troy used his thumbs and fingers with devastating skill, pinching her nipples lightly until he had her squirming. The hard length pressed between her legs became more apparent every minute. It was perfect, and wonderful, and oh my *God*, hard to breathe, but she needed one thing to be clear.

"I get to reinstate talking time whenever I want," she warned.

"We need to add a naked rule to talk time, to keep things rolling." He grabbed the bottom of her shirt and peeled it upward, stripping it over her head as she lifted her arms to help. Her clothes were abandoned to the floor, Troy hummed his approval. He returned his hands to cup her ass, lifting her gently as he brought her forward to use his tongue.

"I'm all for that tradition," Nic gasped. "Except it will make public conversations a little awkward."

She clutched his shoulders as he swirled his tongue around her nipples until they glistened.

"People can look away. Or watch. I don't fucking care."

He put his mouth over her entire nipple and sucked, his hands trembling as she arched toward him, instinctively trying to get closer. She wanted to crawl into him and never leave.

Nicole had imagined that they'd be going slow today, but the longer he touched her, the less that seemed like a good thing.

Troy seemed to have the same idea, thank goodness, scrambling for the button and zipper on her jeans, shoving the material off her hips. Only when she would have stepped back to lose them completely, he forced her to stop. He hauled her onto the couch, one foot on either side of his hips, her jeans bunched around one ankle.

"Oh God, *Troy*..."

He ignored her protests and brought her forward to his mouth, going from zero to a hundred in an instant. Tongue slamming into her body as he gripped her ass and held her in place. Teasing along one side, then the other, before focusing all of his attention on her clit.

Her legs shook as he licked, tongue rasping over sensitive nerves. Her legs quivered when he paused. "Don't worry, sweetheart. I won't stop until you've come at least a couple times.

Nicole clutched his head for balance, the room whirling around her. Heat stormed throughout her system, a tight ball of pleasure flashing wider and wider with every caress until her sex tightened down around emptiness.

The wave of her orgasm rushed over her, barely ebbing before he went back to work, slower this time, harder. Flicking his tongue faster and faster as the pressure built up and up until there was nowhere to go except with the explosion.

Nicole moaned as he moved his mouth away, holding her legs until she was steady.

"My turn," he said, drawing her attention downward as he brought her lower.

"Holy cow. When did you...?" Nic gasped as his cock bumped into tender skin.

"We'll go slow," he promised, guiding the head of his cock between her legs as she hovered over him. "Take your time, babe, but I'm going to fill you up good."

His eyes—mesmerizing as he stared back. One thick inch at a time slipped into her as she rocked up and down. "Did I pass out for a bit?" she asked. "I swear you didn't have time to get out your cock, let alone put on a condom.

"Desperation drives a man to amazing heights," he offered, his lashes fluttering up for a second as she took him nearly all the way into her body. "*Jeez*, that's so fucking good."

She hummed in agreement, regaining enough strength

to turn it into a "torment Troy" moment. Small pulses, over and over. Just the head of his cock enveloped in her heat as she grew wetter. Troy held her breasts in his hands, leaning in at every opportunity to steal a lick. Or pinching and teasing until she was so distracted she hadn't realized the small teases had given way to full-out strokes over the length of his cock on every motion.

Thick and hot, his cock stretched her perfectly. Troy caught her hips and took control of the timing, rocking upward as he pulled her down to meet him.

Nicole let her head fall back and pleasure take her again.

Driving deep. Thrusting harder, and harder. Sensation grew then blurred, holding her captive on the edge until she couldn't take it any longer. She called out his name and broke.

This time there was something to hold on to. Something very noticeable and wonderful. Her pussy clenched hard on his length as he continued to pound into her.

"Fuck, Nic. *Yes.* That's it. Squeeze me tight. *Holy—*"

Troy shuddered to a stop, muscles rock-hard as he quivered with the power of his orgasm. Heat and pleasure created a cocoon around them as their naked chests aligned. Connected and shaking, panting for air and grasping to find a way to keep close. Closer still, even. His body inside hers like it was meant to be.

Nicole curled her arms around his shoulders and let him support her. Let him care for her as satisfaction rolled in and over, and left them floating in dreamy contentment.

CHAPTER 14

Nicole pushed through the back door at her sister's, phone against her ear.

"Hey, Laurel, it's Nic. I can't come over. Sorry, but Jodie asked Mike to babysit because Dale's got a meeting tonight, which means I need to pop in and make sure my brother isn't feeding the kids Red Hots or jars of Maraschino cherries."

Her friend's soft laugh rippled over the line. "These are frequent events when Mike babysits?"

"On the good days." Nicole eyed the chaos that had taken over the counter in the kitchen, where the remains of a mac-and-cheese box was still visible, along with way more pots and orange-coated spoons than necessary to feed three small children and one oversized, albeit still *annoying enough to be a kid at heart* brother. "He's a super uncle, which means he buys the noisiest toys on the shelf. You know, the type who wires the kids up before he heads home."

"I did that last year," Laurel confessed. "The noisy-toy thing. I regret it now that I'm home. All those bells and whistles drive me crazy, even during the short visits to my sister's."

"Yeah, me too."

A shocking silence lay over the entire house. The dining room table was covered in empty dishes. Stray macaroni noodles clung to the bowls, while a few remaining carrots and celery sticks and small broccoli florets sprouted from a container of ranch dip. The highchair was coated in a thick layer of something puce-coloured she didn't even want to guess the food source for.

But there was no sign of the kids, or her brother.

"I seem to have lost them," she confessed to Laurel. "I doubt Mike took them outside. It's nearly bedtime."

"Follow your nose," her friend deadpanned. "We're talking three kids under the age of five—someone needs changing if they don't need to be completely hosed off."

Finally something registered. A low rumble from the basement. Moving closer, it was clearly a deep, male voice followed by the excited whisperings of children.

Nicole peeked her head around the corner into the playroom and stopped in shock. Instead of chaos, she discovered her nephews and niece had been magically enchanted into perfect behaviour, but not by her brother.

Troy Thompson had settled his bulk onto the middle of the worn playroom couch. With a kid on either side of him and the baby in his lap, one strong hand cradled Dahlia upright against his chest while his free hand held a children's book. The boys hung over his arms, silence falling as Troy picked up the story again.

Oh, this was so not fair.

Nicole forced herself to look away, rotating until her back was against the wall. "I think my ovaries just exploded," she murmured into her phone.

Silence echoed from the other end of the line for just long enough to make it really clear Laurel was uncomfortable. "Do I...want to know why?"

"Oh, shut up. Mike's not here. *Troy's* babysitting. He's got three kids draped all over him, and he looks happy as a pig in mud."

He looked like he freaking *loved* being surrounded by the kiddies, and the final brick got shoved out of the protective wall she'd built.

Her friend caught on far too fast. "This is where I should say something about karma, except in more religious terms, right?"

"This is where I tell you to take a hike."

Laurel laughed. "Really? Not even a swear word? You *are* turning over a new leaf."

"Don't push me. I'll call you back later."

She chanced another peek. It was worse than she thought. Troy was totally getting into it, growling along with whatever character was in the book. The little boys hid their faces against his shoulders. Dahlia's jaw dropped and she stared up at him, little baby fingers reaching out to touch his face.

He pretended to chew on her until she giggled, and that's when it happened. The worst thing possible.

Troy plucked up the baby and gave her a kiss on the cheek, a look of happy amazement drifting over his features as he cuddled her for a moment before tucking her back into his lap.

Nicole turned away again, body aching in places that shouldn't feel so empty.

He was *not* playing fair.

She snuck up the stairs and went to work cleaning the

mess, mostly because it gave her something to do while her mind raced, trying to make sense of her discovery.

It wasn't finding Troy happily ensconced with her sister's ankle-biters. It was the craving she hadn't expected to feel so strongly while thinking about him in conjunction with kids.

Suddenly the idea of making babies with Troy played out in Technicolor in her brain, and she had to put down the pot in her hands before she dropped it.

Babies with dark eyes and dark hair that curled over their foreheads. Babies with laughter that rang out when their daddy nibbled their toes or tickled their tummies. She knew exactly how pretty Thompson babies could be—little Tanner was dangerously cute.

Add in Troy's sweet side, and mischievous side, and...

Fuck, she was seriously going to fall over and die of a hormone overdose if she kept this up.

The rumbling from the basement got louder. Story time must be over. Nicole gave the table a final wipe before turning to face the top of the stairs.

Tyson and Tucker spotted her first, sweeping in with shouts of "Annie Nic, Annie Nic."

Dark-brown eyes met hers even as she knelt to hug her nephews close. Troy held Dahlia easily in one arm, her little head resting on his chest, eyes drooping closed.

She felt another twist deep inside her gut as she swallowed hard and offered a rather breathless "Hey."

"Hey," he returned. "Okay, guys. Looks like your auntie came to help get you into bed. Who's going to be the first awesome dude ready for good-night kisses?"

Incredibly, it worked, Tucker and Tyson racing off down the hall toward the bathroom.

"Is that like the Pied Piper in reverse? You can convince

them all to run away from you with a single spell?" Nicole asked in amazement.

"Hey, they're no dummies. Beautiful woman offering kisses in bed? I'd be running this instant if I had a bed within sprinting distance."

He tucked her against him, kissing her briefly, Dahlia's warm body between them. It was a teeny taste of heaven, and Nicole shivered with the impact of it, ninety-nine percent sure she was tipping past the point of no return.

Troy pressed Dahlia into her arms. "You want to put her down while I get the varmints ready for you?"

"Meet you in their room in a couple of minutes."

It was scary right and natural to be standing in a house passing a sleepy baby between them. Nicole held Dahlia to her chest as Troy backed away, staring at her with a cocky smile as if he knew *exactly* how hard her hormones were percolating at that moment.

HE'D DELIBERATELY SUGGESTED he'd take Mike's place as babysitter that evening. Partly as an ongoing peace offering to his friend, partly because he needed to know if he could deal with this final hurdle.

Everything else about being with Nic was aces, but with her wanting kids ASAP, he needed to be able to put up or shut up. And now as he supervised tooth brushing and potty duty, he could still hear his friend's droll comments...

"You want to spend an evening with the carpet monsters?" Mike had eyed him suspiciously. "Tell me this is to impress my sister."

"It's to impress your sister."

Mike snorted. "I'm still pissed at you, but not because you're dating her, by the way."

"Am I taking over tonight for you or not?" Troy demanded. "And then you can tell me what's got your wittle fweelings all tangled wup."

"Ass," Mike drawled. "Yes, you can babysit. I'll text Jodie and give her the heads-up. But I'm pissed because you didn't fucking *tell* me."

"Tell you...what?"

Mike pulled out his phone and sent his sister a text. "That you liked Nic for real."

"You said you'd rip my arms off if I ever touched her," Troy reminded him.

"So? That's what any brother would do. Hell, I'm pretty sure you did worse to Gage once upon a time. You're my best friend, you idiot. Even if you are an ass, you're better than most jerks out there. Them, I'd rip their heads off."

"Body parts equal the level of your affections. Got it." Troy sighed. "You're right."

Mike blinked, glancing up from his phone. "Really?"

Troy nodded. "I should have told you, only she wanted us to keep it secret. And when it comes between making you happy, and making Nic happy? She wins. Hands down, every fucking time."

His friend stared at him, his expression brightening. "Now that? Is what I needed to hear months ago. You have my blessing, son."

"Screw you," Troy muttered.

"The rule still stands—don't *ever* talk to me about sex again. Oh, and if I ever catch her crying? It's not your arms or head I'll remove from your body," Mike said evenly.

"Threat?"

"Promise."

Troy had laughed, accepting the brotherly back pounding he'd gotten from his friend, suddenly aware of a load lifting off his shoulders that he hadn't realized had been weighing him down.

He'd missed Mike's friendship.

But just then he wasn't about bromance—he was a man on a mission. He'd shown up at the house, gotten the kid-sitting detail rundown from a moderately hesitant Jodie before she was forced to leave or cancel her evening out.

The ensuing chaos had been…

Well, frankly, it had been a blast. Convincing the little guys to stop running around the house screaming at the top of their lungs had taken him joining in, shouting louder than either Tyson or Tucker as he tore in circles around the coffee table, waving his arms like a banshee.

The boys had been suitably impressed, although Dahlia's lips had quivered for a second as she stared wide-eyed over the edge of the playpen, but he'd dealt with that as well.

Somehow all those puzzles and tricks Nic had played on him over the past months had turned into the perfect rugrat corralling training, and he felt like the king of the world discovering these little people *liked* him.

And now, with the boys climbing under their matching *Star Wars* quilts, and Nic joining him to tuck them in, he nearly quivered with excitement. He had to let her know he was completely on board to have some of their own.

Which…*holy. Fucking. Shit.*

They left the boys' room with nightlights shining, closing the door firmly behind them. Troy caught her fingers, intending to bring her with him to the living room, but she surprised him, tugging him to a halt. Wrapping her fingers around his neck and bringing him in for an eager kiss right there in the hallway.

Her taste was intoxicating the way he'd always imagined strong liquor to be, his concentration spinning as she leaned back on the wall and pulled him over her like a protective layer. Bodies tight together, lips meshing, Troy dragged in gasps of air when he could, hands gripping her hips tightly to stop himself from ripping away the layers between them.

He stumbled them a few steps farther from the kids' rooms. Nic had her hands buried under his shirt and was lightly scratching his back like a cat marking its territory.

The deep, urgent need he felt for her was rising fast, but they couldn't just keep going. Somehow he tugged his lips from hers.

"Talk time," he begged.

Nic groaned dramatically, melting against him for a moment as her forehead dropped to his chest. Both of them were breathing hard, and it took a moment before they made it to vertical. She blew out a long, slow breath then guided him back to the living room.

It seemed the safest thing to drop into the armchair and put a little distance between them. At least that was Troy's idea.

Nic's was to lower herself into his lap the instant he sat down.

He fought to keep the growl from his voice as he spoke. "You're not making it easy to keep things PG."

"You *never* make it easy," she confessed, but she relented and switched to the couch, staring across the three feet separating them as if it was the Grand Canyon. "So. Talk time?"

Hell if he could remember what he wanted to tell her. "Right."

Her pulse pounded in her neck, and he wanted to press his lips to the spot. To lick it then move up her neck to the sensitive spot under her ear. All the while he'd be removing her clothes until he could lay himself over her and—

"Oh my God, will you *stop* that?" The corners of her lips lifted in a smile, the surface wet from having dragged her tongue over them.

"Stop what?" He could picture her. Naked and open before him. Lying back on the couch, one foot up, her pussy—

A needy sound escaped her. "I'm going to explode if you keep looking at me like that."

He tore his gaze away, glancing down the hall. All was quiet on the kiddie front. Didn't mean it would stay that way, but to hell with it. A little clean fooling around would ease his cravings until they were really alone.

Troy shot to his feet and closed the distance between them, dropping onto the couch beside her. "Here. I'll sit where you can't see my face."

He clicked on the TV, changed it to some renovation show, and adjusted the volume so it wouldn't disturb the kids.

"Troy?"

He stretched his arm along the top of the couch behind her. "I changed my mind. We'll talk later. Watch the show," he ordered.

Nic wiggled briefly, but slowly relaxed, leaning her body against his. She lowered a hand to his thigh, eyes locked on the screen.

Troy leaned over and nuzzled the side of her neck. "I love how soft you are here," he whispered. "No, keep your eyes on the show. I'm going to touch you, and you're going keep facing the TV, no matter what."

A shiver shook her the slightest bit, and he reined in the urge to shout his approval. Perfect woman. So fucking perfect for him.

He caught her earlobe between his teeth and bit down before dragging it into his mouth. Teasing her ear with his tongue until her fingers tightened on his thigh and she squirmed in place.

"Can I—?"

"No," he whispered. "No talking. No questions. Just feel."

He grabbed her shirt, tugging the fabric free to press his palm to her warm belly. Stroking in circles as he moved in on her lips. Kissing her again, accepting her mouth moving under his and the little gasps of pleasure and her moan of approval as he pushed her bra out of the way to get at her breast.

She snuck her hand farther into his lap. An innocent enough move, but completely on purpose. Her lips curved into a smile he felt against his mouth.

Especially when the pressure of her palm increased, rubbing vertically over his rock-solid length.

"Minx," he muttered, but it was too good to order her to stop. So they sat there, blue light of the TV flickering in the background as they made out on the couch like two teenage kids afraid to go any further.

Hands caressing, teeth nipping. Little groans escaping as they adjusted position over and over, never enough and yet all they could—

The back door rattled, and they scrambled apart, the teenage sensation far too realistic.

"I'm home. Nicole? Did I see your car out there? Troy? Everything okay?"

Jodie's voice, ergo Jodie, was getting closer far too quickly.

"We're here in the living room. No troubles," Nic called.

Giggles escaped as she fought to straighten her clothes, which set Troy laughing silently as he attempted to help her and just got in the way. She batted at his hands, so he bounced to his feet, wishing like hell he'd thought to grab a pillow to hold in front of him as Nic's sister rounded the corner and took in the scene, storm clouds forming instantly on her face.

"What exactly is going on here?" Ice dripped from every word.

Troy hesitated. He wasn't sure how to answer, so he kind of ignored the question and instead went into a recap. "Kids went down fine about thirty minutes ago. Dahlia didn't finish her supper, but she drank her entire bottle, and all of them brushed their teeth. Well, I helped Dahlia. No troubles at all to report."

Jodie stared for a moment before stomping down the hall without a word to peek into the kids' rooms.

Nic joined him at his side, her clothing finally back in place, and she squeezed his fingers briefly, opening her mouth to share with her sister. "I got here about—"

"One sec," Jodie interrupted, turning to face Troy, her expression unreadable. "Thanks for watching them. I'd like to talk to my sister, if you don't mind."

Troy shrugged. "No prob."

"*Alone.*"

Nicole sighed. "Go on, I'll meet you outside," she whispered at Troy.

"You going to get grounded?" he whispered back. "I'll stay and take my punishment with you."

She tapped him with her elbow toward the door, the weight of Jodie's disapproval rising by the minute. "Go. It'll just be a minute."

There was not much he could do, so he stepped outside, but not out of earshot, dismay rising as Jodie let loose the instant he was out of sight.

"I can't believe you would do this." Jodie's horror and disgust was clear, even in the hushed tones.

"What did we do?" Nic demanded. "You're overreacting. We weren't rolling around naked, having sex on the floor. There was nothing shocking happening that would've warped the kids if they'd gotten out of bed."

"But you were supposed to be *babysitting*," her sister whispered furiously. "That means staying attentive and keeping your clothes on."

"My clothes were on," Nic said. Jodie must have given her a look or something because Nic caved. "Okay, fine, *mostly* on."

"Just go home," Jodie snapped.

A low growl escaped Nicole. "Are you telling me every time the kids are in bed, you're attentive one hundred percent of the time?"

"It's different when you're babysitting."

Nic refused to drop it. "And you never *ever* take your clothes off when the kids are asleep?" Dead silence before Nic made a rude noise. "I feel damn sorry for Dale, and I have no idea how you got pregnant three times—"

"That's enough. I've had enough of you, and I've had more than enough of that...*Troy*. Get out of here."

Troy waited until she joined him, slipping his fingers into hers and guiding her toward her car. Silence hovered as they stood there, her door open, night air swirling around them.

Nic let out a huge sigh.

Troy's guilt did double time. Everything that had been amusing about the situation vanished. "I'm sorry."

She paused, one hand on the open car door, shock in her eyes. "What for?"

He shrugged. "She's right. I promised I'd take care of the kids. I shouldn't have been fooling around with you."

"Oh, for fuck's sake." She caught him by the coat front and jerked him closer, fire in her eyes. "You listen to me, Troy Thompson. We didn't do anything wrong. My sister is being a *jackass*. Those kids thoroughly enjoyed you being their babysitter tonight instead of Mike."

Guilt still rippled. "I don't want your family mad at you."

"She'll get over it," Nic promised, smoothing her hands down his chest and pressing a sweet kiss to the side of his neck. "Want to come home with me?"

More than anything, but something was very not right. "I think I'll go home. I'll see you tomorrow."

The hurt in her eyes only added to the guilt washing over him in waves. It was a cold, lonely drive home as his conscience haunted him. How could he need someone so much, and yet be so wrong for her?

The ache in his heart grew another notch.

By the time he made it to the parking lot outside his apartment, he still didn't know what to do with himself. He was restless. Aching.

He sat in his car and stared out the front window like the biggest loser on earth, all his previous good intentions and confidence wiped away. He wanted the best for Nic, even if that meant walking away from her. It would be like ripping out his heart and leaving it behind.

He didn't know if he was strong enough to give her up. To give up all the dreams he'd finally thought within reach.

A light tap sounded on the window beside him, and he shook himself alert, opening the door in confusion to discover Nic peering down at him.

"Shove over," she ordered. "I'm taking you for a ride."

CHAPTER 15

Certain moments in Nicole's life shone with crystal clarity. Like back in eighth grade when she'd realized her supposedly best friend *wasn't*. Or when she'd figured out sex was something people did for fun.

Eye opening, to say the least.

Revelation hit hard moments after Troy drove off and left her, his confusion and sadness clear. They'd been having so much fun together moments earlier. That night they'd connected on a new, deeper level, she was *sure* of it.

The only thing that had changed between sweet laughter in the living room and him driving away upset had been Jodie's disapproving comments. Clearly that was what had distressed Troy, and that was what she needed to fix. Now, before they lost something precious.

Nicole loved her family madly, but that didn't make them the be all and end all when it came to what was right for her or her future. They still had issues with Troy? Tough. She had none...and it was time to damn well tell him that.

He made it easy for her to stalk him by waiting in his

truck, and now he stared at her, his eyes looking far more lost than usual.

She hung on to the doorframe, raising one brow. "You going to move this century?"

He gave in, sliding across the bench seat to let her get behind the wheel. "I don't get to ride shotgun very often."

Nicole adjusted the seat so she could reach the gas pedal before patting the space beside her. "I seem to remember some fine young man telling me no way in hell was I allowed to sit all the way over by the window while we were dating."

Troy shook his head in amusement, but he followed her orders, ending back in the middle of the truck. "This doesn't work quite as well for me. My legs are longer than yours."

"Suck it up, sunshine. You can stretch your legs all the way over to the far corner. You keep your ass where it belongs beside me."

She put the car into gear, fighting to keep from laughing at the expression on his face.

"You're a little feisty, aren't you?" Troy commented.

"I haven't even gotten started," she warned.

"We headed somewhere in particular?"

"You'll find out soon enough."

Troy stretched his arms along the back of the seat, turning up the radio and singing along as she aimed the truck out of town to the west. He didn't say anything else until a low chuckle escaped as she took the corner onto a familiar dirt road.

"Why, Ms. Adams. I do suspect you're taking me to Heartbreak Ridge. I'll have you know I'm not that kind of a man."

"I know *exactly* what kind of a man you are," Nicole promised. "Trust me."

A full-out snicker escaped him. "Just the tip? Is that what you're saying?"

She snorted. "You're terrible."

He wrapped his fingers around the back of her neck, a strong caress that dug deep into her muscles as he twisted sideways and offered a grin. "If you're really determined, you *might* be able to talk me into something."

"I'm pretty sure about that." Nicole slowed the truck, taking the bumpy route cautiously as she aimed for a spot equal distance between the two vehicles already overlooking the Red Deer River.

She put the truck into park, pushed Troy into the passenger seat then wiggled out from behind the wheel so they were facing each other full on.

He'd gone quiet as he stroked the hair back from her face. "I'm sorry for ditching you. Just had a lot on my mind, and I wasn't sure I would be good company anymore tonight."

"Obviously, I either don't care or have a different opinion." Nicole caught his fingers in hers. Fighting to find the right words. It was all good and well to tell herself she was going to make the situation clear between them, but simply blurting it out seemed wrong.

Then again, screw it. Why make things more complicated than they needed to be?

"I like you," she confessed.

His lips twitched. "Awwww. I like you too."

"And that's what matters." She examined him closely. "When you were all into messing up my speed-dating evening—"

"I beg your pardon. I did no such thing."

"Yeah, yeah. You were a perfect gentleman and

followed every one of the rules. *Not.* Shut up and let me lecture you."

"Yes, ma'am." He stole a kiss though, and something flickered inside her chest. Hope?

"As I was saying, when you sat there and told me I needed to be taking a serious look at you as a boyfriend, I thought you were being your normal pain in the ass, but you weren't."

"I was being extraordinary—?"

She jammed her hand over his mouth to make him be quiet. "You said you were right for me, and it's true. You *are* exactly who I need in my life, Troy Thompson."

The crease formed between his brows. "Then why do you sound so sad when you say that?"

"Because I need to know if... Okay, this is going to get a little complicated."

He leaned against the seat back, arm stretched past her. "Hey. Don't look so serious. We don't have to do this tonight. We're okay, really."

Nicole was determined to make him understand, and she didn't want to wait any longer. "Remember all those puzzles we did over the years? All the mixed-up games we played when no one else was looking, between toys and puns and other tricks?"

He nodded, curiosity rising.

"Over the past while, I've been struggling to figure out the puzzle that is Troy Thompson."

He laughed. "Okay, that's not what I expected you to say. I'm not very complicated," he insisted.

"That's what you like to pretend. Heck, maybe it's even what you believe, but I think I've solved you. Or I'm ninety-nine percent of the way there."

His grin grew wider. "Hey, if it makes you happy, you can untangle my pieces all you want, sweetheart."

"I will." She held up fingers as she spoke, counting off items. "You played football to make your dad happy. You don't want your brothers to know the things you did for them because 'they're in the past'. But the more I think about it the more I remember seeing you doing things, like letting Clay mother you, and going wild and crazy with Mitch. But with Len you're a lot quieter, and around Katy, you work like crazy to make her laugh."

His gaze was fixed on her. "They're my family. I care about them a lot."

"I know you do. You're everything to everyone because you love them. That's why Katy called you a rainbow."

"I'm a rainbow? Were you drinking at the time?"

"No, she was telling me about seeing people like colours. And you? You go around matching people's colours. That's why everyone in this damn town likes you even if they think you've made less than stellar choices."

His lips twitched. "Thanks. I think."

She shook her head. "It doesn't matter what they think, because every choice you've made has been on someone else's behalf, hasn't it? To please the people you care about. You're a rainbow, Troy, because you're so busy trying to do what makes other people happy that you never do what *you* want."

This time he didn't have a smart answer.

Nicole wiggled until she was kneeling on the seat, reaching up to cup his face in her palms. "What do you want, Troy? What is going to make *your* colour shine through instead of reflecting everyone else's?"

"Why is this so important, as weirdly fascinating as it is to talk about rainbows?"

She took her future happiness up with both hands and laid it out before him.

"Because, while you're exactly who I need in my life, am *I* who you need?" Nicole lowered her voice, forcing the words out past a throat gone tight. "I don't want you to settle for anything other than what's best for *you*. It's too important. So I need to know—what do you really want, Troy?"

It took a second before understanding cleared his eyes. And then she couldn't see his expression because he'd hauled her into his lap and was kissing her senseless.

A possessive grip took hold of the back of her neck as he kept their lips in firm contact. Another hand dropped to her lower back, pressing their torsos together as she settled into his lap. It wasn't quite the answer she'd expected, but it was definitive and nothing she was about to argue with.

Although it did make it difficult for her to tell him she loved him when they had their tongues in each other's mouths.

Troy Thompson held on tight as the most frickin' amazing miracle occurred. Everything he wanted was right there in his lap. She'd damn near broken him in two with her honesty and the fear he'd seen on her face. Worried that he'd reject her—

Bullshit on that. How could he survive without his heart?

Tap, tap, tap, tap.

For the second time that night, he nearly jumped out of his skin at the clatter of knuckles on the window only inches from his ear.

He didn't think they'd been kissing that long, but the

windows were steamed up, fuzzing the bright light shining in his eyes. Nicole scrambled off his lap and back into the driver's seat as Troy cursed and hit the window control, rolling it partway down.

"Oh, *hell*." A familiar female voice.

Troy blinked hard, holding up a hand to block the light. "*Anna?*"

His sister-in-law swung the flashlight away, bending over to lean on the window ledge and peek into the truck. "What is it with you, Troy Thompson? Didn't get parking out of your system back when you were fifteen?"

"I promise he's here of his own free will, Officer," Nicole said clearly, drawing Anna's attention. "I won't use the ropes in the back until we get home.

Anna shook her head, stifling her laughter. "I swear I should get danger pay for having to deal nonstop with *both* the Thompson and Coleman clans. You two okay?"

"I was better a few minutes ago before you interrupted us," Troy grumbled.

Nicole elbowed him in the side as she leaned across and smiled sweetly at Anna. "Is this when you suggest we find somewhere else to fool around?"

"Please. Since you *both* have homes to go to."

"You don't need to sound so smug," Troy said.

"Yes, I do. It's in my job description." Anna leaned down once more and spoke over Troy. "Hey, Nic. Will I see you later this week at the Thompson family dinner?"

"Wouldn't miss it," Nicole promised. "Janey said you're bringing dessert?"

"S'mores. About the extent of my baking skills."

Troy fought to keep from laughing as the girls kept chatting.

"Never mind me," he muttered. "I'll just sit here and

listen to my sister-in-law the cop and my girlfriend discuss next week's dinner while everyone around us wonders what we're getting arrested for."

"*Shhhh*," Anna and Nicole ordered at the same time, and Troy lost it, laughing out loud as he pushed open his door and strolled around to the driver's side.

Nic slid over, and by the time he got behind the wheel, the girls were done their conversation, waving goodbye as he backed the truck out carefully. He waggled his fingers at Anna then headed toward Rocky.

He and Nic sat in muted silence for all of thirty seconds before she laughed. Low at first, growing stronger. Addictive. Contagious. Troy caved and joined in. He had to pull over to the side of the road to avoid going into the ditch.

"Oh my God, I can't breathe," Nic gasped.

"Can't see. Stop it," Troy demanded, wiping at his eyes, which just set her off harder.

It took a while for them to calm down to the point he could suck in a lungful of air and put the truck back in drive. They both trembled on the edge of going off all over again, and he stared determinedly at the road until temptation passed.

"My face hurts from smiling," Nic boasted when he pulled into the parking space behind her house.

He flashed another grin her way then met her on the path, linking their fingers together and kissing her knuckles. "Now. Where were we before we were so *rudely* interrupted?"

Nic twisted on the spot, walking backward as she led him to the house and up the steps. "You were about to let me have my wicked way with you."

"Perfect. You should get naked and do that."

"Yes, sir."

She stripped off her shirt and let it fall. It pooled into a bright blue puddle on the top step of stairs, and she stood there in the fading twilight, smooth skin glowing in the faint echo of streetlights reaching the backyard.

"Babe, you're beautiful."

Her eyes flashed, sexual hunger and something *else* slamming into him as she blew him a kiss.

She crooked a finger. "Follow me..."

He moved slowly, letting her get ahead of him as the striptease continued. Through the living room and down the hall...

Pants abandoned by the recliner.

Her lacey bra hooked precariously on the edge of a picture frame.

Barely-there panties dangled from the doorknob of her bedroom.

Troy pushed open the door all the way, standing in the doorway to take in the view.

Nic was in the process of crawling onto the bed, her naked ass toward him...

...Wonder Woman socks on her feet.

So fucking perfect.

She rolled, propping herself against the pillows as he closed the distance between them to stand beside the mattress, gazing down to enjoy every exposed inch.

Nic smiled as she reached for her socks.

"Leave them on," he ordered.

"Kinky." She put her hands on her shins and dragged them up her body until she was stretched out before him.

"Anything we want. If it makes us happy, it's a go." Troy stripped off his shirt, tossing it aside before popping open the button on his jeans and partially opening his zipper.

Just to relieve the damn pressure before the top of his head blew skyward.

"You make me happy," Nic whispered. "You're perfect for me."

Her gaze slipped over him, hot and needy. Pride trickled up his spine. This woman had picked him as who she wanted. He needed her to know he'd damn well picked her as well.

Now and forever.

For *everything*. Every fucking thing she'd dreamed of, and a whole lot they'd never even thought of yet.

He paused and considered. It needed to be said clearly, so she'd never have any doubts. "I want *you*. Fine, I'm a fucking rainbow. It's how I show love, and I'll probably keep being one because that's who I am. But even rainbows need the sunshine to bring out their magic, and that's you, baby. You're the one who makes me shine."

Her eyes—so amazing. Fixed on him, full of fire and emotion.

"I don't want you to have to pick between me and your family," he admitted. The last barrier standing.

She shook her head. "I won't have to. But Troy? If I *did* have to pick?" She knelt forward so she could touch him, laying her hand on his chest, directly over his heart. Her voice soft and sincere. "It's not even a question. I'd pick you. Every time."

Joy swelled inside him. He leaned forward, crawling over her as Nicole settled against the mattress. Lips connecting, his torso pressed to hers. Slow languid kisses as if they had all night. All week...

A lifetime.

She murmured something against his lips, rolling them to the side as her hands pressed at his jeans. He helped her take them off, digging into the back pocket for the condom he'd put there before she tossed the fabric to the floor.

Then he pulled her back into his arms. Touching and caressing. Hands on her breasts, lifting them to his mouth. Licking and sucking until she squirmed under him.

He slid a hand over her torso until he reached her sex, cupping her possessively.

Troy pulled back just far enough to look into her green eyes. "Feel. Feel me loving you."

He pressed a single finger between her folds and stroked. Teasing her clit in circles as he stared into her face and watched pleasure sweep in. She curled a hand behind his neck, panting as she grew closer to the edge. Holding on tight as he took her higher.

Her lashes fluttered closed as she breathed out his name, and he rolled between her thighs, pressing his cock into her still-pulsing body. Liquid heat surrounded him, pleasure streaking up his spine like a lightning bolt as she widened her legs and welcomed him in.

Buried to the hilt, Troy steadied his breathing, braced over her on his elbows. Nicole wrapped her legs around him, the socks digging into his butt making them both smile.

"I love you," he said softly.

Her eyes widened.

"I love *you*," he tried again before she could speak, louder this time. "I. Fucking. *Love*. You."

He punctuated every word with a kiss on her smiling lips.

"I love you too. I think I always have." Nicole dragged her fingers over his shoulders, scratching lightly. "Love me now?"

"Now and always," he promised, rocking forward. Slowly, over and over again.

It seemed as if there'd always been an element of desperation to sex before—as if they'd been trying to get in as much pleasure as possible before it all vanished.

Now he knew they had forever. She wasn't going to vanish. She wasn't going to leave him for someone else, and this time their lovemaking seemed deeper. More intimate.

Even as he picked up the pace, sinking into her harder, she held him tenderly and stared at him with love in her eyes.

He reached between their bodies and touched her clit, stroking on every thrust as moans of desire escaped them, unstoppable.

Pleasure struck between one breath and the next.

"*Troy...*"

Nic thrashed beneath him, her legs a vice holding him in place as her body squeezed his cock. He angled his hips to go as deep as possible as he lost control and gave in to the ecstasy driving through him.

"Hell, *yes.*" She sighed deeply and collapsed into a boneless mass under him.

He chuckled, rolling to the side and pulling her tight against him.

For a split second, fear that he'd disappoint her at some point in the future snuck in, but he banished the negative thoughts. She knew him—she loved *him.* Imperfect as he was.

No matter what it took, he was going to make sure she never regretted picking him.

He nuzzled against her throat and said it all over. "I love you."

She answered with a kiss and a slow, wicked caress that sent his blood racing again. "Of course you do," she said, squeezing his butt again. "We need some naked talk time. Here, or in the shower?"

Troy outright laughed, picking her up and rolling to his feet. "I pick the kitchen."

"Oh, now we're getting kinky." Nic clutched his neck and grinned as he carried her down the hallway. "I guess you never did get to do me on the dining room table."

Fuck. His body was halfway back to loaded already.

"You really are perfect for me," he said as he lowered her to the sturdy table and started all over again.

CHAPTER 16

Troy: *got a surprise 4 you*

 Nic: *a nice surprise? ;)*

  Troy: *dirty girl. I always have nice things for you*

Nic: *tell me!!!!*

Troy: *nope*

Nic: *spill. Don't make me hurt you*

Troy: *meet me @ Traders @ 7*

Nic: *K*

Troy: *parking lot*

Nic: *?????*

Troy: *you're gonna <# this*

Nic: *lol! LICK*

Troy: *lmao I meant <3*

Nic: *it's ice cream!*

Troy: *it's perfect, just like you*

Nic: *awww. Tell me!!!!!*

Troy: *nope*

Troy: *have to wait*

Troy: *<#*

. . .

THAT WAS ALL SHE GOT, but it was enough to have her smiling in anticipation.

Two weeks since they'd spent far more than seven minutes in heaven, and she still grinned every time that night replayed in her mind. Which it did regularly, much to everyone in her vicinity's chagrin.

They were waiting for Mike to find a new roommate or a smaller apartment, but plans for moving in together were in motion. *Life* was in motion—they were taking the next steps. Together.

Nicole could barely believe how damn happy she was, even if everything wasn't perfect. Her family...needed more time.

Laurel poked her in the arm, and Nicole pulled her attention back to her friend. "Are you done? They're going to wipe down the table and sweep us away with the crumbs."

Nicole blinked hard, focusing on the pale blonde across the table from her at the café. "Sorry. Daydreaming."

"Really? I never noticed," Laurel deadpanned. "Let me just remove these spider webs from where they've sprung up to forever connect you to the café."

"Shut up," Nicole mumbled, but she rose and left the restaurant, walking back to work with Laurel at her side. "Are you finally going to join us for dancing tonight at Traders?"

"That's a definite positive maybe."

"*Laurel*," Nicole wheedled. "I'll introduce you to Chase..."

"Sure. Now that you've found your match in Troy,

you've tossed aside your leftovers like so much discarded candy."

God. "He's not my leftovers. Stop that."

Laurel flashed a grin. "I promise I'll come with you sometime, but not tonight."

"I wish you'd get yourself a hot date," Nicole said seriously.

"I wish I would too, but alas, pyrotechnic humanoids are not yet savvy to the joys of earth prime."

Nicole looked her over with concern. "Were you drinking during lunch, and I didn't notice?"

"Never mind. I obviously read a broader range of material than you do."

"That's for sure." Nicole gave her a quick hug then headed into work, diving into her tasks to distract herself from whatever Troy had planned for the evening.

Time dragged like never before.

Draaaaaaaaagggggggged.

She checked her phone a dozen times between lunch and getting home, but there were no more messages. She resisted texting him—the man would only tease her for being impatient, and he'd be right.

It wasn't *her* fault she was in the parking lot at six forty-five, trying to look blasé as she sat on the rustic bench outside the dance-floor door. She waved at friends as they slipped past, chatted with a few, and considered hiding when Mike showed up just after seven.

He paused. Looked around. "Where's the ball and chain?"

Nicole offered her best annoyed-sister expression. "Meeting me here."

Mike frowned. "I didn't see him at the apartment after work. What's he doing?"

"That's for me to find out and then tell you," Nicole said.

He snorted, waving as he headed inside. "See you when he shows up, then."

"Sure." She leaned back on the bench, turning her face toward the sun as she kicked her feet lazily. Every now and then she checked her watch, trying not to let her curiosity send her impatience rising too fast.

Still, when she checked the time and it was seven thirty, she couldn't resist sending a text.

No answer.

And no answer to her phone call, either. It went to voice mail, and Nicole stared down the road in confusion. She even went back and read through the texts he'd sent earlier in the day, in case she'd made a mistake.

When eight o'clock rolled around with no sign of Troy, she was past worried. With one final glance over her shoulder, she made her way inside and found Mike.

Her brother was on the dance floor and not too pleased to discover her tugging on his shoulder. "What?"

"Troy's late."

"He's an asshole," Mike shouted over the music. "Thanks for telling me."

When he would have gone back to dancing, she tugged harder, offering his dance partner an apologetic glance. "*Mike.*"

He looked totally hard done by before dipping his head toward the other woman. "Sorry, sweets, my sister's boyfriend needs me to track him down and run him over with my truck."

She laughed and blew him a kiss.

Mike was still pouting when they hit the front door. Nicole scoured the parking lot in the hopes Troy had shown up while she'd been gone, but no luck. She hauled out her phone and checked it again.

"What the heck is going on?" Mike demanded.

"Troy said he'd be here at seven, and it's way later than that. And I can't get hold of him, either."

"So he forgot. He's being a jerk. What do you want me to do?"

Nicole growled at her twin. "He's not a jerk. He said he'd be here, and he's over an hour late."

Mike hauled out his phone and made a call. He waited then shrugged. "He's not answering, but I'm sure he's fine. Hell, his phone is probably dead or something stupid."

That made sense. A dead phone was a completely plausible explanation for everything—except why Troy wasn't here. Her sick sensation of worry was growing by the second. "You're coming with me," Nicole ordered.

"What? No way." Mike shook his head. "I'm going back into Traders and—

She caught him by the shirtfront and got into his face. "You're coming with me until we damn well find out what's *wrong.*"

Her twin sighed, but he marched into the parking lot with Nicole hard on his heels. "Sure. Whatever. But when we find him at the apartment with his feet up on the coffee table, eating pizza and drinking rootbeer, you owe me big time."

"Deal." By now the sense of foreboding was so strong she hoped she'd have to pay the forfeit.

But the lights were out at the apartment, and there was no sign Troy had come home after work, his truck nowhere to be seen.

Mike tried to look relaxed, but he was fighting a losing

battle as well. "He must have gotten held up at work. I'll call the shop."

His expression tightened only a minute later.

"Answering machine?" Nicole asked.

"Yeah. Closed for the day. You got the numbers for any of the Thompson gang?" When she nodded, he pulled her toward the door. "Let's hit the garage. You can call the Thompsons on the way. I'm sure it's nothing."

But he didn't sound as nonchalant as before, the two of them rushing down the stairs back to his truck. Mike drove in silence as Nicole phoned Katy and Janey, getting confused negative responses from both of them.

Katy offered to make more calls. "I'll check with Clay and Mitch, and call you back the instant I know anything, but I'm looking out the window now at the shop, and I don't see Troy's truck where he usually parks it."

"Thanks. I'm sorry for calling out of the blue—"

"Nicole Adams, stop that. I'd lose my shit if Gage were this late for no reason. We'll figure it out."

Nicole wanted to hug Katy hard. "Thanks."

Mike waited until she'd given him an update. "Okay— what exactly did Troy tell you?"

"That he had a surprise for me and would meet me at Traders."

"Okay, long shot. Call Mom and the girls, just in case his surprise somehow involved them, and he got waylaid."

Nicole bent over her phone, fingers flying over the screen. She took the time to shoot a text at Laurel first.

Nic: *favour*

Laurel: *yo*

Nic: *Troy's AWOL. Supposed 2 meet me @ Traders. Worried. Tracking him down. Can you go wait there in case he shows up?*

Laurel: *of course*

Laurel: *praying, if you're not offended by that idea*

At that moment? Nothing could offend her.

At least that's what Nicole thought until she got negative responses from all her family. Including Jodie, who had the *bullshit* idea of using the moment to make a smart-ass comment.

"Get used to being treated like this," she warned.

Nicole stiffened. "What does *that* mean?"

"He'd obviously taken off and forgot to tell you. Probably went out drinking. It's no big deal to him, because he's not responsible—"

Nicole hung up, really wishing she had an app that would have amplified the sound and volume of her displeasure. Something equivalent to a door slamming in her sister's stupid face.

Mike was white knuckling the steering wheel. "Anything?"

"Nothing, except Jodie needs an ass kicking."

The lights were out at the Thompson and Sons garage. Nicole raced up the back stairs and banged on the door to the bachelor apartment over the shop.

Mr. Thompson opened the door, his smile growing as he noticed Mike standing behind her. "Hey, it's the trouble twins. Good to see—"

"Do you know where Troy is?" Nicole blurted out.

Keith shrugged. "No. Why?"

"He's missing,"

"Ha. Hiding on you, is he?"

She shook her head, annoyed at having to proclaim this all over. "No. He was supposed to meet me over an hour and a half ago, and we can't get hold of him."

Keith paused. "We can check the appointment book if you'd like. Maybe he got called on an emergency? Is the tow truck in the yard? He's supposed to—"

Nicole ignored whatever Keith had to say, whirling on the spot. Mike was already taking the stairs two at a time to the ground level, sprinting around the side of the building where the tow trucks were stored.

He jerked to a halt in plain sight, shaking his head at her. "Both trucks are here," he shouted.

By the time she got down to his level, more vehicles were pulling into the yard as the Thompsons descended en masse. Troy's oldest brother was the first to reach her, asking the same questions all over regarding his message.

She was getting desperate to *do* something. "I know it doesn't seem like a long time, but I swear—Troy's not goofing around. Something's wrong or he would have been there. Or he'd have gotten in touch with me. I *know* it."

Clay nodded slowly.

Anger flared. "He's not slacking off somewhere," she all but shouted. "If Maggie called Troy to say *you* were this late, he'd already be out looking for you. No questions asked."

"Hey, it's going to be okay." Clay caught her in a bear hug and squeezed her tight. "I'm not doubting you, I'm trying to plan the best thing to do first."

She gave in for a moment, accepting the comfort of a strong embrace. But once she got moving, she didn't expect to stop until she found the missing piece of her heart.

Clay gestured his family closer as he spoke to Nicole. "Sounds like he went to pick up something for you. He must have gotten stuck somewhere along the way—even mechanics can break down, and if his phone was dead, he'd wait with his truck for us to find him." He patted her arm reassuringly then turned to his brothers. "I didn't notice. When did Troy leave work?"

"He took off early. Said he had to hit the bank." Len frowned. "Which means he's been gone since three."

Oh my God. Nicole's stomach plummeted even further.

Mitch stepped forward. "I just called Anna. She said he's not in the lockup at the station"—he held a hand toward Nicole to stop her defensive retort—"not that I expected him to be. She says we need to check the hospital, medi-centres, and all his usual hangouts before she can do anything official police-like."

Hospital. Nicole felt the blood draining from her head, and the yard started to spin.

Clay caught hold of her arm. "Hey. We'll find him."

Janey had her phone out now. "I'll text my friend Shannon. She's on shift at the hospital. She'll check intake records for us."

Clay nodded. "Let's make a list and divide it up. The sooner we find him, the better."

The guys went to work while Nicole strengthened her resolve. Somewhere out there, Troy needed help. He was damn well going to get it. Every bit of help she could muster, even if it meant knocking sense into some family with less than stellar attitudes.

She called Kevin and Cyndi's first.

Her sister answered without even a hello. "Jeez, Nic. What the heck did you do to Jodie? She's flipping out about how rude—"

"Let me talk to Kevin," Nicole ordered.

"What am I? Chopped—?"

"Now, Cyndi, or you'll regret it."

"Fine."

The next voice on the line was her brother-in-law's. "Nic?"

"Troy is missing. We're organizing search parties, and I need you and Dale ready to go as soon as we have an area for you to check out. Don't ask anything more than 'what can I do to help', or I swear I'll disown the lot of you in a fucking second."

She had to give him credit for taking her threat seriously. "I'm grabbing my keys. I'll call Dale and Brian. You want me to phone anyone else?"

Sheer relief made her head spin. "I'll let you know."

"You okay, sugar? You need Cyndi to come give you a hand?"

"I'm going looking with the crews. Tell her to stay home with the babies."

"We love you, Nic. It's going to be okay."

His confident statement went a long way to easing the frustrations of having to threaten her family in the first place. Right now, she didn't care what it took. All she wanted was wheels on the ground looking for Troy.

No...all she wanted was *Troy*, found, and in one healthy piece.

Maybe Laurel was rubbing off on her because she found herself damn near praying as everyone headed in different directions.

Katy caught her by the arm before she and Mike hit the truck. "If Troy took money out from the bank, I might be able to find out something to help us. He gave me all his passwords and banking information last year. Said he wanted someone to be a backup."

Nicole nodded even as tears threatened. Trust Troy to give his information to the one family member who most needed to know he trusted them, in spite of Katy's issues with numbers. "If you find anything—"

"I'll call right away," Katy promised.

Gage and Katy stayed behind with Mr. Thompson as a base for everyone to check in with. A sleepy Tanner lay curled up against his daddy's chest as Gage leaned over a table covered with maps.

Mike drove, and Nicole stared out the window at the darkening sky. Lights shone from behind the tall garage doors, the building lit up with an unnatural-looking brilliance for the time of night. It was just shy of nine o'clock, and the sun had already gone behind the mountains, streaks of colour reaching toward the heavens.

On any other night it would have been beautiful. Now the beauty was washed away by the knowledge it was going to be pitch-black within the hour.

"We'll find him," Mike promised. "He's going to be okay."

"He will," she said with as much conviction as possible. Nicole faced her brother. "Thank you for not suggesting we check with past girlfriends."

"He's not cheating on you, Nic. He'd *never* do that."

"Still, thank you."

"The guy loves you. Hell, I suppose it makes sense. You *are* my sister, after all. You must be pretty amazing."

He offered the weak attempt at a joke, and she took it, hanging on to the seat with both hands and praying.

Hang on, Troy, I'm coming to get you.

P ain.

    Intense, *through his entire body, making it hard to breathe* pain.

It was the only reference point Troy had for the first few moments before he sucked in enough air to allow a hoarse groan to escape.

He opened his eyes, blinking into the darkness. It took a moment for his vision to adjust, but even when faint shadows appeared, everything beyond his immediate area was pitch-black and eerily quiet.

Troy took stock, deliberately slowing his breathing. He used every relaxation technique he'd learned during his days on the field, flexing one body part at a time to check if any were in desperate condition.

The worst of it was a short list, thank God. His rib cage and chest throbbed with pain, and his right shin. His head hurt like the devil, and when he reached up, it was clear he was bleeding —stickiness coated his fingers as he touched the side of his face.

The weirdest bit was he didn't seem to be sitting on the

level. Instead, he hung twisted sideways, the seatbelt holding him partially suspended in midair.

A few more things came into focus. The airbag hung from the center of the steering wheel, the deflated pink material like a gory after-party decoration gone wrong...

Oh hell, he'd gone off the road.

"*Jeez.*"

Troy thought back, working hard to pin the scrambled details into order. It had been early afternoon when he'd picked up the certified cheque and the transport insurance he needed before heading out to Maxwell Kent's.

It had taken him a steady week to convince Max to sell him the car, every bit of his golden-boy charm in play. In the end he'd come clean and told the truth...

"I NEED it as an engagement gift for my girl."

"You're settling down?" Maxwell's bushy brows rose, followed by a wink. "The Adams girl, is it?"

"Yes, sir." Troy flashed his most enticing grin. "I think she'll have me, but if I sweeten the pot with the car, I *know* she will..."

Max laughed. "Go on with you. The girl would be lucky to have you, with or without the car. But...okay. I guess I can give her up now." He swept a hand over the hood. "I've been taking her out regular," he confessed, "just to keep her in running order. My son would have liked that."

"If you're willing, we'll come by and take you for a spin now and then," Troy offered. He would have suggested Maxwell could drive, but the man would probably enjoy the company as much as anything else.

The older man nodded, and it was clear he was pleased. "That'd be fine."

The Mustang was in amazing shape for how long it had been off the road. Troy had come out a couple days in a row to go over the entire vehicle carefully. Sneaking around without letting Nic figure out what was going on had been sheer murder, but it was so going to be worth it to see the expression on her face when he pulled in at Traders.

Or at least...that *had* been the plan.

Troy glanced around at what had been a pretty nice vehicle. Now the door beside him was crumpled, the front windshield a web of cracks barely visible in the pale light. Overhead, a branch stuck through the convertible roof, the sturdy material peeled back and fluttering in the light wind like tissue paper.

So much for Nic's fancy you-deserve-to-be-spoiled present.

Troy swore. And swore again. Searching his memory for what had happened.

He pressed a hand over his forehead, gingerly touching the solid lump he found there, rising like a baseball. Great— he probably had a concussion to go with the rest of his broken parts.

And something was definitely broken. He'd gotten bruised ribs after being tackled on the field. This was worse, by a long shot.

He twisted in the seat, stopping as soon as his ribs protested in a full-out scream. The car sat at an angle, nose down, passenger side lower than where he was pinned in position.

There seemed to be a lot of trees around the vehicle. And *over* the car—it was as if he'd been buried under a bonfire pile. Troy peered into the dim lighting, trying to figure out the lay of the land. The only other landmark was the steep shadowed slope of a hill visible behind him outside the mass of trees.

Turning his head far enough to see that much made stars dance in his vision.

He lifted a hand to check his watch—the light came on, the numbers clear and bright. 6:57.

Damn it, he was going to be late.

He wiggled to the side, freezing instantly as what felt like daggers thrust through his body. Okay—so he wasn't going to try *that* again. He patted his pockets carefully, wondering where the hell his phone had gone.

Troy removed his watch, using it as a flashlight to search around him. Everything that had been loose had ended up on the passenger floor, including bits and pieces of the Mustang that had broken free and now sat in a chaotic heap he couldn't reach.

He bet his phone was somewhere in there.

The only thing he could snag was the sleeve of his jacket—it had caught on the stick shift—and he pulled it loose, gratefully draping the fabric over his torso. Shock was going to hit soon, and staying warm would help ease the stress.

Unlocking the seatbelt would let him free, but with his leg pinned and everything else that hurt, Troy wasn't sure that was the best idea.

He closed his eyes, thinking back. He'd given Maxwell the cheque, then arranged to leave his truck in the barn overnight or until Nic could drive him out to grab it.

He'd done a final systems check on everything, shooting the breeze with Maxwell who'd hung around the entire time. Troy ended up having dinner with the man—it had been impossible to say no, and he didn't have anywhere to be until seven, anyway.

On the highway, headed to town...

Thinking hurt. Troy took more deep breaths, picturing the road. Picturing the curve and the—

—trucker in his lane.

Shit. Troy tightened at the memory, then swore again because tightening up fucking *hurt*.

There'd been an eighteen-wheeler in his lane, and he'd had nowhere to go but to the right to avoid being hit head on. And to the right was a steep embankment. He was damn lucky the car hadn't rolled—there must have been enough undergrowth to give him a surface to slide down, and enough trees to jerk the car to a stop.

Now the rest made sense. If he'd passed out, it hadn't been for long.

It was frustrating as anything to be trapped, with no way to get himself free, and no way to call for help. He leaned on where the horn should be, and nothing happened. The front of the car was crushed enough to have cut or dislodged the horn wiring.

He was stuck until someone found him, and considering where he was, that didn't sound like good odds.

Screw this. He'd just found the love of his life. He had plans, dammit, plans he desperately wanted to accomplish. Like waking up beside Nic every morning, and having babies with her, and all the rest.

He was not going to curl up and die alone in some ravine. Not without trying everything possible. Nic had asked him what he really, truly wanted—and he knew the answer. He wanted a lifetime with her.

Troy reached for the seatbelt and braced himself.

"WAIT, you're breaking up. Let me get a stronger signal, and I'll call you back." Nicole grabbed Mike's arm, hope rushing in over the solid layer of fear she'd been fighting for the past hour. "Head toward town—Katy thinks she's got something for us."

"Done." He pulled a U-turn.

Nicole watched the signal bars on her phone flicker between zero and one bar and cursed all rural cell towers.

The instant she got two bars she hit redial. "Drive a bit more, but we should be good."

"Nic?" Excitement brightened Katy's voice. "I know where Troy was this afternoon."

"Really?"

"His bank records show a withdrawal to motor vehicles, so insurance, and a certified cheque to Maxwell Kent."

Oh my God. "He bought the convertible."

"Which means he's probably on the side of the road— I'm sorry I didn't figure this out earlier." Katy sounded miserable.

"Are you kidding me? You're amazing. Troy's going to be so pleased you figured it out at all. Bank stuff is tough." Nic covered the phone. "Head to Maxwell Kent's," she ordered her brother before getting back on with Katy. "Can you look up Max's number for me?"

"One step ahead of you. Gage is talking to him right now. One sec—"

Mike was turning on to the secondary highway headed toward the Kent's farm. "Nic?"

"In a minute," she warned. "I'm waiting for Gage."

He was on the line in seconds.

"Maxwell says Troy left around six thirty, which doesn't

give him time to go anywhere else if he wanted to be at Traders by the top of the hour. He's got to be on that road," Gage assured her. "I'll call the rest of the crew and head them your way."

"If we find him with his feet up on the dash, we'll let you know right away," she promised.

Mike waited until she'd lowered the phone. "Update."

"He was at Maxwell's until six thirty, so keep your eyes peeled for turn outs, in case he pulled off the road to do repairs and he's stuck."

The trip to the farm passed too quickly—there was no sign of Troy at all. Nicole peered into the darkness, every sense on high alert for the sight that never arrived.

Mike drove them past Maxwell's barn, turning in a circle to shine his headlights on all the possible parking spaces, but no miracle occurred. No one jumped out to reassure her, although Maxwell was making his way from the front porch.

Mike stared into the empty field ahead of them. "This makes no sense."

"Turn around," Nicole ordered.

"But we drove—"

"Turn the damn truck around," she repeated, each word etched in thicker ice the longer it took him to move, "or get your ass out and I'll drive myself. He's out there, Mike. Somewhere."

"Okay. I know. It's just crazy. How can a car disappear?"

"It *can't*, so we missed something."

Maxwell held up a hand and Mike lowered his window.

Nicole was ready to crawl out and start running down the highway if this took too long.

Luckily, Maxwell just handed them an oversized flashlight. "Thought this might help. Let me know when you find him."

Mike took off, and they headed back down the highway. Nicole made him turn on his blinkers so they could inch their way along the road as she poked her head out the open window, shining the flashlight into the ditch.

Her brother phoned Gage to update him, hanging up to let Nicole know the latest. "The others are starting from town, going slower this time, just like us."

Slow. Painfully slow when every bit of her wanted to rush. A rock stuck in the wheel well rattled over and over until she was ready to scream.

She wanted to see him. Needed to tell him how much she loved him. How much forever was going to rock because they were together. Nicole didn't allow her mind to drift toward anything other than the option that they'd find him in one piece—waiting for her.

The phone resting on the console between them went off, and she and Mike both jumped a foot into the air as she scrambled to answer it.

"Hello?"

"Nic, we found him. Mile 17." It was her brother-in-law Kevin. "He's down the ditch, but I've got my fire team here. We're getting him up the embankment, and there's already an ambulance on the way."

Her hands were shaking so hard she could barely hold the phone. "He's okay?"

"He will be," Kevin promised. "Tell Mike not to rush— you'll be here before they take him away."

The short time it took to relay the message and travel the distance back toward town seemed impossibly long. Flashing lights were everywhere, trucks turned to face into the ravine. Nicole realized they were shining their headlamps into the darkness to allow the rescue team to see what they were doing.

"Don't you jump out before I stop," Mike warned. "Troy will kick your ass if you get hurt doing something stupid."

The instant he put the truck in park she was out the door and running, cautiously after that warning, but still as fast as possible toward the action.

The fire crew had hold of a rope and were steadily climbing the steep embankment, a spinal board supported between them.

"Oh my God." The words whispered out, but she kept moving toward the edge. "Troy? *Troy?*" Louder the second time. Loud enough to hear the fear in her own voice.

"Hey, baby. I'm a little tied down at the moment."

The sound of his laid-back drawl nearly did her in. She met the board at the edge of the road, fighting tears because her bursting into a sobbing mess was the last thing he needed right now. "Look at you, lazy butt. How did you rate the harem to carry you around?"

"Don't they look great? I'm thinking of getting them to hang around 24/7. Especially the big blond—I might hire him to give me piggyback rides."

The big blond—Chase—chuckled. "Of course, Your Majesty. Although I hope you don't try to steer…"

Troy hissed. "Low-blow, man, low-blow. I'll have you know I ended up exactly where I intended."

They were carrying him toward the ambulance, and Nicole could only catch glimpses of his face. "I'll meet you at the hospital," she promised.

"Sure." Troy lifted a hand from the board. "Hey, Nic?"

"Yeah?"

"I love you. Sorry I crashed your car."

Plain as day, straight up, a hint of amusement in his voice.

How she found the strength to imitate his casual tone, she had no idea. "I love you too. We'll buy another. Or maybe a tank."

He wiggled his fingers. "See you in a bit. Oh, and tell Mike he needs to bring in his truck sometime soon—his brake pads need replacing."

Then he was gone into the back of the ambulance.

Nicole turned, the smile she'd pinned in place vanishing between one breath and the next. Choking on tears of relief as strong hands wrapped around her shoulders and pulled her against a solid chest.

Kevin. "He's going to be okay, Nic. We found him in time."

"Good." She sucked for air around the tears. "I need to get to the hospital. Where's Mike?"

"Right here." Her brother caught her by the hand and led her back to the truck. "Come on, let's get you there in one piece."

It was a long enough ride she let herself cry for a bit before wiping her eyes and getting herself under control. Until she saw Troy up close and personal, and knew he was really truly okay, she wasn't going to believe it.

Mike dropped her by the emergency doors. "I'll park then join you."

Emergency staff made her wait until the trauma-room nurses said she could go in, guiding her down narrow hallways into the triage area.

Troy lay on a semi-reclined bed, IV drip inserted in his left arm, while a doctor worked a row of stitches on his head.

Of course, he spotted her before she could say anything. "Hey beautiful."

"Looks who's talking, handsome." There was room beside the bed near his hip, and Nicole slipped into the space. She caught his fingers in hers, holding them cautiously.

He reassured her with a strong squeeze. "I hear I'm the main event for a while, Nic. Stitches, X-rays..."

"Ultrasound," the nurse added, turning to Nicole. "You can stay here, or wait in the main area."

"I'll stay."

"They finished my leg before you got here," Troy told her proudly. "Double layer of stitches on that one."

"Fancy. Did you get the embroidery option?"

He made a sound halfway between a laugh and a grunt. "And...we won't do that for a bit. Laughing hurts."

Damn it, she was an idiot. "Sorry."

"Don't be. I love you exactly the way you are. Hang around, and I'll find a closet for us."

She was not going to cry, dammit. "I plan on sticking around for as long as you'll let me."

Their gazes met, and an emotional storm hit—more powerful than being wrapped up in the middle of a wild session of sex.

He'd heard what she was saying. Heard it either in her voice, or maybe it was osmosis between their fingers. They were *it*. Together, through everything.

The expression in his eyes was enough to help get her through the uncertainty and fear of the next couple of hours as they hauled him out for more tests before returning him to wait for results.

The nursing staff had to be keeping the rest of the family away—it was the only explanation Nicole could think of for there not being a mess of Thompsons surrounding them.

Although, at one point Clay appeared at her elbow, glancing around at the empty floor inside their curtained area. "Are you hanging in there?"

"Yeah. I need to sneak out for a pit stop." She rubbed weary eyes, but there was no way in hell she was going home until Troy was settled.

Clay pressed a brotherly kiss to her temple. "I'll stick around until you get back. In case Troy shows up."

Nicole found the nearest washroom, barely noticing how hellish she looked in the mirror. She washed up, splashing icy-cold water on her face and the back of her neck.

She felt partially human again by the time she headed back to emergency, jerking to a stop at the sight of an empty bed. Two new nurses were changing the sheets, and Nicole clung to the doorframe and willed herself to stay vertical.

He was fine. Troy was *fine*.

Oh my God, where was he?

"Nic." Solid hands on her shoulders.

She whirled, looking into Clay's face. "Troy?"

"He's been moved to another room. They're keeping him overnight for observation because of the bump to his head. Come on, I'll show you where he is."

It was a good thing Clay took her by the arm, because all the air drained from her lungs at once.

Of *course* they'd moved Troy during the five-minute window she'd stepped away. Someday Nicole planned to have a short, violent talk with Fate about how it wasn't funny to jerk people around like that.

Clay led her to Troy's bedside. "I'll stick around. Drive you home when you're ready."

"I'm staying," Nicole insisted, linking her fingers with Troy's as she examined his face carefully.

"It's okay for you to go," Troy said. "They gave me a shot and a half of something that's making me pretty damn relaxed. I'm going to be out like a light in a few minutes."

"Still staying."

Troy glanced past her. "You heard her, bro. Arguing with the lady is futile."

Clay pointed a finger at her. "Phone if you change your mind."

The room went quiet when he left, Nicole's throat tight all over again as she carefully leaned in and stroked Troy's face. "You scared me," she confessed.

"I scared me too," he admitted. "But everything's going to be fine. Well, except for the Mustang. Damn shame about her."

Nicole bit back tears. "She wasn't ready to come out of retirement."

"No, I guess not." Troy lifted her hand to his mouth and kissed her knuckles. "You saved me."

For the first time he wasn't laughing or lighthearted. It was pure adoration she heard in his voice.

"You need to sleep."

"No." He kissed her hand again. "I need you to know that you saved my life, and I'm so damn grateful. I mean, I hurt like a bugger, or I will when the joy juice wears off, but a few broken parts and some stitches are nothing compared to what would have happened if you hadn't gotten everyone moving."

"You were late," she said. "I was worried."

"You saved me," he repeated. "No one's ever saved me before. I wouldn't have lasted the night out there, Nic. Clay said you were something else, ready to take on the world until they got their asses in gear."

The hours since she'd sat waiting at Traders were a blur... Had she really?

"Honestly? I don't even remember that. I just knew something was wrong." *Oh hell.* "Laurel—I left her waiting at Traders in case you showed up there."

"She'll be fine." Troy tugged her closer. "You saved me, and now you're stuck with me. That's how it works, right? You save someone, and they're yours forever."

Sounded good to her, if she could talk without losing it.

He hummed softly, stroking her fingers. "Kiss me, baby. And seriously, you can go home."

Nicole gently pressed her lips to his with as much love as she could. "I *am* home," she whispered.

He was already asleep.

EPILOGUE

November, Rocky Mountain House

Two months had passed since the accident, and Troy had recovered rapidly. Nicole figured it was because he was in such good shape to begin with, and stubborn to boot. He'd begun taking walks the day after he'd been released. Heck, he would have gone back to work if his family hadn't loudly vetoed the idea.

They'd managed to keep him out of the shop for all of two weeks.

Troy claimed his rapid recovery was from sex, which he reinitiated far sooner than she thought possible. The man was nothing if not determined.

And clever.

"I'll let you do all the work," he'd murmured, running a hand over her hip as she cleaned up after dinner. "I promise, I'll lie there and stay as still as possible. Just think—you can be in control for once."

He kissed her neck and sent shivers racing down her spine. "*Troy...*"

"Honestly, the only thing that hurts right now is my cock," he complained, sneaking behind her and tugging their bodies together. "We've already done the hand-job thing. And oral. Do your magic, baby. Make my day."

Of course, she'd given in, and the slow, careful love-making that had followed had been incredible.

Now, a month after that first time, they weren't quite as cautious, although not completely up to their old enthusiasm level. Still, the session they'd just finished left both of them lying flat out on the bed, sated and content. Fingers linked as they panted for air.

Troy rolled toward her, lazily tracing a finger down her body. "That was awesome. Again?"

"You're terrible," Nicole teased.

"I'm *your* terrible." He pressed a kiss to her collarbone. "I like living here with you, and it's a cozy house, but we should look into something bigger for down the road."

A shiver of excitement raced over her. So many changes since the accident—

No, not changes.

Confirmations.

Things they'd already decided now advancing to the next stage. Troy had moved in with her when he'd been released from the hospital. Said he wasn't going to spend another night apart.

And their lovemaking? No condoms.

A mix of joy and fear struck. They could end up starting their family at any time, and...Troy had been right. Even eager as she was, the nine months it would take for a baby to arrive would give her time to get her head in gear.

In the meantime, they had each other to enjoy and a future to plan for. At Nicole's insistence, Troy had looked into colleges and training programs he could partially complete through correspondence. Whether babies arrived sooner or later—both of them were in complete agreement that Troy was going to train for a new career.

The look in his eyes as she'd sat with him while he filled in application forms to become a personal trainer had made *her* want to jump up and start dancing. But the expression on his face when he'd gotten the acceptance letter to his first choice had been even better—

He was scheduled to start in January.

"I got hold of Maxwell Kent," Troy shared, staring at her like she was made of the most exquisite chocolate and he was about to take a long lick.

"Did he say when he planned on cashing the cheque?" They'd been waiting for the money to be pulled from Troy's account. Having it unaccounted for made the accountant side of her twitch.

"Yup. Never."

"What?" Nicole sat up in shock. "That makes no sense."

Troy shrugged. "He said he plans to pretend the car is still in his field, so he doesn't want the money. And I should go buy you another car."

"He can't do that," Nicole said, confusion hitting hard. "Can he do that?"

"It's his choice, baby. Let the man be generous if he wants." Troy stroked her again. "So, what colour car do I need to find?"

She pressed a hand to his chest. "I don't need that car."

"I know. I still want you to have it." He winked, but didn't say any more.

That had been a few days earlier, but she'd been thinking about it as she fell asleep, Troy's strong arm draped over her body. The man had something up his sleeve—that was obvious. For someone who still surprised her with his spontaneity, he was getting pretty good at making plans as well.

Something clattered, and she jerked awake, groggy and confused.

The noise sounded again, this time from the closed window.

"Troy? Something's outside." She reached across the bed toward where he'd been curled against her.

He wasn't there.

She sat up, confused, looking around the room that was dimly lit with the pale light of dawn. "Troy?"

It was six thirty in the morning, and he wasn't where he was supposed to be and something was—

Clink.

Clink.

Nicole scrambled out of bed and peered out the window as another *clink* sounded.

Someone was standing on the snowy lawn and was throwing pebbles at the window. Not someone—Troy.

She shoved open the window. "What the heck are you doing?"

He dropped to his knees and threw open his arms. "Oh, fair Rapunzel, let down... No, wait. Wrong lines."

She snickered. "I think so. Ain't no way you're climbing my hair to get in this window."

"That's okay, I can get in the window without it." He pushed himself up on the open window ledge so he was on level with her.

"That's cheating, you know. Climbing in first-storey windows isn't that impressive."

Troy grinned. "Your fault for not having a two-storey house."

"What are you doing? Come back to bed," Nicole said,

tugging on his jacket.

"Get dressed and join me," he countered. "I have a surprise for you."

She paused. "The last time you said that, it didn't end well."

He was all the way in the room and tossing clothes at her. "It ended fine. We're together. Get dressed, and get moving."

There was no arguing with him when he was in this mood, and she wasn't going to try.

"Fine, but I'm walking out the front door, not crawling out the window," she warned.

Troy? Didn't say a word. Just waited until she was dressed and pulled on her boots and then he gave the biggest puppy-dog eyes ever...

Nicole growled. "You are the most wonderfully annoying person I know, Troy Thompson. It's a good thing I love you."

Then she climbed out the damn window, letting Troy help her to the ground.

By now streaks of light were brightening the sky, and she held Troy's hand and let him lead her where he wanted, which seemed to be around the side of the house to the back where...

...a shiny blue Mustang waited in her parking space.

"Holy shit—you *didn't*."

"I did." Troy pulled keys from his pocket and shook them. "I've been waiting two months for this moment."

But instead of handing them to her, he pulled her into his arms, tipped her head back and kissed her soundly.

When he finally let her go, Nicole was grinning from ear to ear. "Forget the car, give me more of those kisses, please."

"I'll do both, but first, Nicole Adams?"

He paused, and her heart skipped a beat at the expression on his face. The complete and utter fascination. The longing.

"Yes?"

Troy's gaze held her in place. "Will you elope with me?"

Oh God. It was so *him*, she burst out laughing. "Elope? Not *get married*?"

"Elope, as in this minute, right now. Weddings suck, remember?"

It wasn't what she'd expected, but it was perfect because it was Troy, and he was everything she needed. "Sure. Love to."

They were in the car, the two of them grinning like fools, headed down the road before she could worry about anything remotely like details. She figured Troy had a plan, or if not, they'd make it up as they went along...

Only when he pulled to a stop outside a wire fence blocking what was not much more than a snowy path leading onto ranching land, she glanced at him in confusion. "Troy?"

"Trust me."

He left the car to open the gate, then drove along the snow-packed route toward the rise of the hill.

Ahead of them the sun continued its slow journey skyward, orange and gold streaks growing stronger.

They topped the ridge and Nicole gasped.

A mass of people stood waiting in a semicircle, battery-operated candles in hands. Tall pillars lined the perimeter, each one supporting another enormous candle and turning the area into an impromptu wedding hall set in a hollow on the ridge.

She twisted to face Troy. "Eloping?"

He grinned as he put the Mustang in park. "Well, the 'right now' part of eloping. I couldn't imagine us getting hitched without our family and friends there."

"Everyone is..." Nicole's throat tightened, and she used the minute it took for him to walk to her door to get herself under control. He offered his hand to bring her to her feet. She went all the way into his arms. "I love you so damn much," she confessed.

"I know." He lifted her hand and kissed her knuckles as he stared into her eyes. "Official sunrise is in fifteen minutes."

"Then we'd better get moving."

"Oh, hang on." Troy reached under his coat and pulled out toques. His with a long jester tail, hers with a crown trimming the top peak.

Both of them rainbow colours.

Nicole laughed. "Really?"

"You going to argue with me?"

Was she going to argue with him? Probably, but not about this. "It's a lovely wedding outfit," she said, taking the toque and slipping it over her head. She adjusted his to fit more rakishly, the long tail draped over his shoulder. Snickers of amusement escaped her at his mock-serious expression.

Laughter. It was going to be a big part of their future— might as well officially start on the right foot.

Surprise sunrise ceremony—when they'd started their fling last January, Troy had no idea this was where they'd end up.

Yet here they were. The woman he loved more than his next breath held his hand as they paced between two massive glowing pillars, all their friends and family gathered around. Wide grins spread across every face as Troy and Nic made their way to the front, where the justice of the peace waited to hear their vows.

It had been one wild ride, but this was exactly where they were meant to be, and Troy wasn't going to miss a second of the adventure.

He took the time to scan the crowd, meeting individual gazes for a meaningful exchange before going to the next. Friends waved their candles. Some offered a nod or a wink, like Kevin and Cyndi. Mike gave them thumbs up. Laurel stepped forward to give Nicole a collection of lace snowflakes on long stems, bundled up like a glittering bouquet of winter flowers.

Short. Sweet.

But with others, it was as if an entire lifetime passed between them in that short moment of connection.

Len smiled, silent as always, but he tipped his chin as if in thanks as he reached an arm around Janey and held her tight. Troy's little sister Katy leaned against Gage, the front of her winter coat swelling over her growing belly. Tanner clutched his daddy's neck with one arm, the other furry mittened hand wrapped around his candle.

Mitch stood next to Anna, and Troy grinned harder as he took in their contrasting outfits. Anna wore full RCMP uniform, Mitch—full biker gear.

They'd announced they were expecting this past week at the Thompson family dinner. The bedlam had been deafening, especially since Clay and Maggie had made the same announcement just a couple weeks earlier.

Troy met his oldest brother's gaze, and damn if Clay didn't swallow hard, as if he was holding back his emotions.

Oh, hell, no. Troy was not going to lose it right now. This was a fucking *happy* moment. He squeezed Nicole's fingers tight, centering himself on her.

Her bright smile grounded him as they continued the slow march forward. Nicole looked past him into the gathering, searching faces as well. His father, her parents...Jodie and Dale.

Jodie, who had all but fallen over herself to make amends over the past months. Having them over to visit, spending time getting to know him better. Troy had waited it out, and in the end he knew Nicole was relieved at the obvious attitude adjustment in her sister. In fact, Jodie had gotten up hours ago to make sure everything was ready for this morning's ceremony, and she'd offered their home for a celebration breakfast afterward.

Whatever awkwardness might have existed was gone, erased like a brilliant winter sunrise after a chilling storm.

Nicole tugged on his hand. "We're here, sweetie."

He turned his attention to where it belonged for the rest of his life, pulling off Nicole's gloves to enfold her bare hands in his. Troy looked into her eyes, and everyone around them faded away. She was beautiful and mesmerizing, but more than that.

She was laughter and light and all that he needed.

Her lips curved into a smile as the justice of the peace raised his voice. "We're here this morning to celebrate. A new day begins, and a new start for Troy and Nicole. New, in that they're making a commitment in front of us. The love they share has been growing for a long time. We don't need to follow any formula to make this official, so I'm going to turn this over to them."

Troy was up, and it still seemed as if they were completely alone, even surrounded with so much family.

"Nic, I threw this at you, so I didn't plan a lot of fancy words. I figured what was in our hearts was the most important part. Plus, we should probably spend more time talking going forward than worrying about what we say at this moment."

"Talk time?" Nicole said with a mischievous smile, and Troy burst out laughing.

"Lots and lots of talk time."

"Sounds good to me." Nicole glanced into the sky. "Do we have a deadline?"

"No. No deadlines, ever. This is you and me, forever, sweetheart." He brushed his thumb over her cheek. "I love you."

Her eyes sparkled. "I love you too. Forever."

It wasn't him who moved first, and it wasn't her. They kind of flowed toward each other, wrapping together and making contact.

Their lips met in what was a surprisingly sweet kiss considering it was them, but what wasn't a surprise was the cheer that rose into the air. Family, friends—shouting their names and congratulations.

Nicole tilted her head and offered a brilliant smile. "Does this make it official?"

"As far as I'm concerned, hell yeah." Troy turned them to face the crowd. "Hey, everyone. I'd like you to meet my wife, Nicole Thompson."

His wife. Holy shit.

Troy glanced back at her. "My light."

Sunrise burst into full view right there in his arms, and it was perfect.

New York Times Bestselling Author Vivian Arend
brings you a sexy and emotional series set in the foothills of
the Alberta Rockies. Meet the Thompsons—five siblings
with secrets and dreams. Join them as each member of this
tight-knit family discovers love.

Thompson & Sons
Ride Baby Ride
Rocky Ride
One Sexy Ride
Let It Ride
A Wild Ride

ABOUT THE AUTHOR

With over 2.5 million books sold, Vivian Arend is a New York Times and USA Today bestselling author of over 60 contemporary and paranormal romance books, including the Six Pack Ranch and Granite Lake Wolves.

Her books are all standalone reads with no cliffhangers. They're humorous yet emotional, with sexy-times and happily-ever-afters. Vivian pretty much thinks she's got the best job in the world, and she's looking forward to giving readers more HEAs. She lives in B.C. Canada with her husband of many years and a fluffy attack Shih-tzu named Luna who ignores everyone except when treats are deployed.

www.vivianarend.com

www.ingramcontent.com/pod-product-compliance
Lightning Source LLC
Chambersburg PA
CBHW021315190726
48288CB00003B/850